'Delightfully black-hearted . . . Not since Flannery O'Connor has a woman writer come along who seems to so thoroughly understand the greasy inner cogs of the male psyche, especially where matters of sex are concerned' Jim Hander, *Baltimore Sun*

'A truly engrossing book . . . told masterfully by a writer seemingly wise beyond her years' Charles Wyrick, *Bookpage*

'She has succeeded in creating a narrative that seamlessly blends the sarcastic and the sincere, the comic and the tragic. Her journalistic eye for the telling detail, her pitch-perfect ear for the lunacies of contemporary speech, her knack for capturing the subtext of hope and memory and regret that informs so many familial exchanges – all combine to make a stylish and spirited debut' Michiko Kakutani, *The New York Times*

'Like Martin Amis and Will Self, Heller is as much a cultural critic as a fiction writer . . . full of sly cultural commentary levelled at the decadent lifestyle of the media types, the Hollywood types and the rich and famous at large' Veronica Scrol, *Booklist*

'She can be nimble, hilarious. She has a shrewd ear for dialogue and conjures a terrific cast of supporting characters' Jeff Giles, *The New York Times Book Review*

'A smashing success . . . Wickedly funny, lively, and – ultimately – moving. Her ability to engage us with a reprehensible, mercilessly biting man is a wonder' Heller McAlpin, *Newsday*

Everything You Know

Zoë Heller

PENGUIN BOOKS

PENGUIN BOOKS

Published by the Penguin Group
Penguin Books Ltd, 80 Strand, London WC2R ORL, England
Penguin Group (USA) Inc., 375 Hudson Street, New York, New York 10014, USA
Penguin Group (Canada), 10 Alcorn Avenue, Toronto, Ontario, Canada M4V 3B2
(a division of Pearson Penguin Canada Inc.)
Penguin Ireland, 25 St Stephen's Green, Dublin 2, Ireland
(a division of Penguin Books Ltd)
Penguin Group (Australia), 250 Camberwell Road, Camberwell, Victoria 3124, Australia
(a division of Pearson Australia Group Pty Ltd)
Penguin Books India Pvt Ltd, 11 Community Centre, Panchsheel Park, New Delhi – 110 017, India
Penguin Group (NZ), cnr Airborne and Rosedale Roads, Albany, Auckland 1310, New Zealand
(a division of Pearson New Zealand Ltd)
Penguin Books (South Africa) (Pty) Ltd, 24 Sturdee Avenue, Rosebank 2196, South Africa

Penguin Books Ltd, Registered Offices: 80 Strand, London WC2R ORL, England

www.penguin.com

First published by Viking 1999
Published in Penguin Books 2000

1

Copyright © Zoe Heller, 1999

'Man with the Blues' by Willie Nelson, copyright © 1975 Glad Music Co., Houston, Texas
77014. All rights internationally reserved. 'Will You Love Me Tomorrow?', words and music
by Gerry Goffin and Carole King, copyright © 1960 Screen Gems–EMI Music Inc., USA.
Reproduced by permission of Screen Gems–EMI Music Ltd, London WC2H OEA

Printed in Englnd by Clays Ltd, St Ives plc

If you need some advice on being lonely
If you need a little help in feeling blue
If you need some advice on how to cry all night
Come to me, I'm the man with the blues.

I'm the man with 100,000 heartaches
And I've got most any colour of the blues
So if you need a little shove in fouling up in love
Come to me, I'm the man with the blues.

Willie Nelson

I

This afternoon, as I came awake from one of those thin, unrefreshing hospital naps, a strange woman was standing over my bed. She was unusually tall – maybe six foot – with a sad, too-long face and a wonky right eye.

'Mr Muller?' she said. 'I hope I didn't disturb you. My name is Vivian Champ. I'm a post-trauma counsellor.'

I shifted slightly, dragging my body up towards the headboard and causing a gust of fuggy air to rise up from the sheets. Vivian's right eye veered about like a restless marble, making her left eye seem peculiarly still and glaring.

'Are you going to give me a bath?' I asked her. (Bathing is a rare and exotic privilege in the modern American hospital regime. In the entire fortnight I have been at the Beverly Memorial, I have been steadfastly refused anything more than a once-a-day wash-down with a chemically moistened cotton-nylon napkin.)

Vivian cocked her head and laughed a tinkling, girlish laugh. 'No, Mr Muller. I'm just here for a chat. How are you feeling?'

There was a short silence while I riffled through a selection of nasty responses and decided, finally, that I couldn't be bothered with any of them.

'I've bought something you might want to listen to,' Vivian said, when it had become clear that I was not going to reply. She produced a cassette tape from her handbag. On its cover there was a line-drawing of two hippy types sitting cross-legged, with their eyes closed. The title of the cassette was *Meditation Chants and Prayers for the Sick*.

'What about a cigarette?' I asked. Vivian smiled at me tolerantly. She wasn't going to be provoked. Smoking is the ultimate no-no here. They'd sooner you shot heroin – they'd sooner you had a bath – than that you partook of tobacco. Early on in my stay, I made a big stink about the no-smoking thing. I threatened a hunger strike. I yelled and made my eyes roll back in my head. I reduced two nurses to tears. But none of this got me a smoke. They're hard, these medical people.

'I don't have anything to play it on,' I told Vivian, gesturing at her tape.

'Don't worry,' she said. 'I can organize a Walkman for you.' She bit at her lips, allowing me a glimpse of her mottled teeth.

'Thank you,' I said, 'but I'm not interested.'

'Why is that?' Her right eyeball seemed to become more agitated.

There was a nervous defiance in her tone that I meant to squash. 'What do you mean, "why"? I'm just not interested. I want a bath.'

She nodded thoughtfully. 'I sense a lot of anger from you. What do you think you are angry about?'

'Look,' I said, with a high, fake laugh. 'I appreciate what you're trying to do for me, but I don't want the tape.'

She nodded again. 'You know, you've been through a very difficult experience. Your main enemy now is stress.'

I had had enough of this ugly person. 'No,' I said. 'No. My main enemy now is *you*.'

Vivian stiffened and blinked. 'This is obviously not a good time,' she said. She put the tape down on my bedside table. 'I'll leave this here for you in case you change your mind.' Then she turned and left. I watched the great, fleshy pistons of her buttocks chug up and down in her nylon slacks as she loped from the room.

Depression and irritability are common symptoms among cardiac patients. My doctor told me so the other day, after I had thrown a stale bagel at one of the Asian trolls who brings me my breakfast. Naturally, I resented his banal diagnosis. *Maybe this has nothing to do with my heart!* I wanted to shout at him. *Maybe I'm having a nervous breakdown!*

All summer I have been feeling fretful, off-kilter – lurching back and forth between deathly exhaustion and manic energy. Work has been a big problem. My pending task is to write the autobiography of Reginald Boon, former king of daytime television. But last year, shortly before I signed on for the Reg-work, my agent managed to sell some producer the film option on my memoir, *To Have and to Hold*, for fifteen grand. And then, when the project got taken on by Curzon Studios, had me hired to write the screenplay for another twenty. This was a pretty good haul for a book that's been sold five times over in the last eight years and a screenplay that, unbeknownst to the studio, has been sitting in my desk drawer for just as long. But thirty-five thousand dollars, when you come down to it, is a most unsatisfactory sum – not nearly enough to allow me to turn down the Boon project and just sufficient to discourage me from doing any work on it. The first draft of Boon was due in two months ago, at the beginning of July. Since June, cushioned by my ill-gotten and rapidly dwindling gains, I have been stuck, revving helplessly, on the tenth sentence of Chapter One. I cannot write a single word. No, that's not true. I can write endless, scabrous fantasies about Boon's family and friends. I can compose scads of pornographic limericks about his boyhood in Idaho. I just can't produce the light-hearted, anecdotal look at the life and times of one of TV-land's greats that is required. Most days, this summer, I have spent collapsed

3

on my sofa, flicking through furniture catalogues and eating cream cheese straight from the tub.

Then, there was the other thing. One morning, two weeks ago, shortly after I had returned from breakfast at the local mall, I received a parcel in the mail from my youngest daughter, Sadie. This was an odd occurrence, because Sadie had not communicated with me – postally or otherwise – for many years. Also, she had been dead for approximately four months.

She died this last May – she killed herself with Mogadons and paracetamols mashed up in Bailey's Irish Cream. A neighbour had been looking after her baby daughter, Pearl, for the night, and when this woman came round the next day to drop the child off, she looked through the letterbox and saw Sadie's blueish leg jutting out from the kitchen on to the hallway lino. Four days afterwards, Sadie was in the ground, buried next to her mother in Highgate Cemetery.

The family made it clear I was not welcome at the funeral, which was fine by me – I wasn't so crazy to attend in any case. (My sister, Monika, rang later to tell me how it went, and apparently the man who did the service referred to Sadie throughout as 'Sody'.) Pearl, now an orphan (her father having absconded shortly after her conception), has been taken to live with her great aunt Margaret in the north of England.

If I am sounding lachrymose or self-pitying, I apologize. The last thing I want to do is whine. Since it happened, I have been busy as a bee, calculating my blessings and registering all the small mercies that were afforded in this instance. Sadie might have done herself in in any number of vulgar or grotesque ways. She might have been a jumper. Or a slasher. She might have hung herself from a light fixture after listening to Satanic messages in pop songs played backwards. As it was, she merely mixed herself a muddy cocktail using a plastic pestle and mortar borrowed from her daughter's Little Miss Chef set. So, lest there be any confusion, let me acknowledge right here: It Could Have Been Worse.

The address on Sadie's parcel had the wrong postcode and the postmark was blurred. Judging from the proliferation of scribbled emendations covering the parcel's brown paper, it had been on a brutal odyssey through the Californian postal system. Luckily, I had never seen Sadie's adult hand-writing before, so I didn't realize straight away that the parcel was from her, and was saved from having a freak-out in front of the postman. My first thought, as I stood there at the door signing for it, was that I had been sent a bomb. I experienced a brief, technicolor vision of exploding fertilizer, raining nails, costly facial reconstruction. And then I saw British stamps, and relaxed. *Oh,* I thought. *Just hate-mail.*

I have been receiving tokens of animosity through the post for eleven years, ever since I was first accused of killing my wife, Oona. In 1970, during a marital spat, Oona broke her skull on a refrigerator door handle and died. I was subsequently convicted of her manslaughter and spent a short time in prison before being found innocent on appeal. The hate-mail comes, as one might expect, from people who approved of the first verdict and were disappointed by the second. Mostly, it is frothy-mouthed, green-ink rants from ladies in Hemel Hempstead. But every now and then I receive oozy, suppurating objects – animal organs, bodily excretions, et cetera. For several months back in 1973, someone in west London express-mailed me a weekly lump of human shit – his or her own, presumably – each one tremulously wrapped in cling-film and silver foil. For five years or so another anonymous enemy kept up a monthly consignment of offal. And there is one tenacious individual who, for nearly a decade now, has specialized in soiled sanitary towels and crumpled paper handkerchiefs caked with snot. I have no strong evidence, but a vibration tells me that the culprit here is my wife's younger sister, Margaret – the one who now has charge of Pearl.

Margaret has always hated me. When Oona and I were newly weds and Margaret was still a social-work student, she used to come and stay with us in London. She would sit knitting in corners, playing the snide country mouse – 'Shop-bought flowers! How grand!' – and moaning about the fact that she couldn't get laid. Later, she press-ganged Bill into marrying her and the two of them went to live in righteous poverty on the outskirts of Leeds. Oona and I once went to visit them on our way to Scotland. Bill made us macaroni cheese for dinner, and afterwards we all had to do the washing-up together while Margaret and Bill sang 'Green Grow the Rushes-o' in rounds. To complete the festive evening, we huddled around their crappy black and white television to watch a general-knowledge quiz hosted by some tweedy English mo. As a special treat, Margaret cracked open a family pack of Cadbury's Fruit & Nut. That's what Margaret is like.

Even though the flow of excrement and other anti-gifts has slacked off somewhat in recent years, I still keep a stock of latex gloves in the kitchen for disposing of the odd Valentine's pig-heart or yuletide phial of vomit. And it was to the kitchen that I went on this occasion, bearing the package gingerly before me. I quickly located the gloves container at the back of a drawer, peeled off a pair and snapped them on. Then I took a knife from the magnetic rack on the wall and began carefully to slice the package open.

Inside, I found three scruffy, ring-bound writing pads and a large white envelope labelled, 'For Pearl'. I sat down, aware that my breathing had become humiliatingly shallow and rapid. Then I opened the envelope and shook out its contents. They were:

a lock of blonde baby hair
a plain silver ring, inscribed with the words, *For SM
  with love, MM*
a pair of baby bootees.

When Sadie died, she did not leave any letters or notes or lipstick scrawls on mirrors to tell everyone why she'd done it. Just herself, palely loitering on her dirty kitchen floor. The absence of any accompanying gloss was a great disappointment to my wife's family. They felt, apparently, that Sadie's omission had denied them closure. Personally, I was relieved. The way most people behave when they know they are about to expire is pretty shabby. It's always the nastiest tyrants who get taken with a mawkish enthusiasm for 'coming to terms' as soon as they know they're going to pop their clogs. Then everyone has to play ball while they lie around in darkened rooms, wheezing fake confessions and clutching their enemies in conciliatory death-cuddles.

I thought Sadie had done exceptionally well to be so efficient and laconic in death. But now, as I trawled through the pathetic items in the envelope, I felt the familiar prickings of parental disappointment. She had succumbed to the sentimentalities of leave-taking, after all. And Christ, isn't life hard enough without that sort of hokey melodrama?

After a while, I opened one of the pads. It appeared to be some rather primitive species of journal. The first page was dated 31 December 1970.

Dear Diary, I read,

Tomorrow is the beginning of the new year and Docter Hume has told me it is helpful to write down my feelings and ideas, so today I am starting a new tradition. Docter Hume has yellow hair and green eyes and is quiet gorgeous. Sophie is quiet infatuated. But first, let me tell you I am nine years old, I have brown hair and brown eyes and my middle name is Sibella after my grandmother on my mums side.

my grandad is called paul. the other grandad is dead and granny Ursula who is my dads mum lives alone behind sainsburys on finchley road. her flat is quiet pokey and she often gets sad because she needs light. My sister is Sophie and she is thirteen. Her middle name is Monika after my aunt. She is very old for her age and quiet obsessed with boys and clothes. Sometimes she is nice to me and tells me her secrets but quiet a lot of the time she is mean and la di da and says o! you wouldn't understand! we live in chalk farm which is near to dingwalls market. Mum who is called Oona died in september and there is quite a controversy about that. now we live just with dad who is called William Muller. He used to be on television. he reported current affairs for a program called 24/7 but he is not working at the moment because he has alot on his plate. He is not as strict as mum. tonight we are going to stay up and see fireworks and watch Drakyula on the telly because even though it is frightening it is a classic. Dad is under alot of strain because he has to meet with lawyers all the time. It is hard for me to make a judgment about dad because I am in the middle of it all. That is why I am having sessions with doctor Hume.

I put down the book. I would like to be able to describe my feelings at this juncture, but I can't really remember them. My actions were as follows: I got up from the table. I took off the latex gloves. I wrapped the latex gloves in a plastic bag and threw them in the bin. I went to my bedroom and changed into my tennis gear. I went back into the kitchen. I ate a slice of roast beef from the refrigerator. I left the house and drove to the Santa Monica Tennis Club, where I met Art Mann, my aforementioned agent. We had completed two sets – both of which, despite strong intimations of nausea, I won – when, at some point shortly after 11 a.m., I had a heart attack.

Heart disease runs in my family, so I had been anticipating this attack for a good twenty years. I had always imagined it as a sharp, knifey thing – the sort of pain that comes with a staccato violin score: *eek, eek, eek*. In the end, though, it wasn't that way at all. It was more like a woozy pummelling in the chest area, and the musical accompaniment wasn't violins, but harp glissandos – the stuff of dream sequences: *mwooah, mwooah, mwooah*. My collapse occurred in the early stages of the third set. I missed a shot, staggered a little, and quite suddenly found myself crawling about the court on hands and knees, feeling unpleasantly wet. (Sweat and some pee, I'm afraid.) Finally, I vomited – producing gobs of that morning's bacon and pancake that sizzled horribly on the hot court tarmac.

My memory grows fuzzy after this point, but I have since been informed that my heart actually stopped for a bit. One of the coaches at the club – some alternative-medicine mo – had me laid out on the court, biting the little finger of my left hand, to get it started again. History doesn't relate what Art was doing while this was going on. I assume he was on a cell phone trying to find out if there was any way we could sue the tennis club.

The next time I became fully conscious, I was in a Cardiac Unit wearing an oxygen mask. Several electrodes on little suckers were attached to my chest and there was a doctor who looked about seventeen years old standing over me, giving instructions to a nurse. Off to one side I could see Art hovering about, eating a bag of fat-free pretzels.

'You had a heart attack,' Art said, spitting shards of pretzel. 'But it's okay. You're going to be fine.'

'No talking, please,' the doctor said sharply.

'Excuse me, Marcus Welby,' Art shouted then, 'this man is my client and my close personal friend. I'll talk to him any damn time I want.' After that, to my immense relief, they ejected him from the ward.

I've been at the Beverly Memorial – or the Bev Mem as it is jauntily referred to around here – for a fortnight now, and I can honestly say it is the filthiest hospital I have ever seen. For years, I have been handing over fiendish monthly sums to some pissy insurance company in preparation for just such a contingency as this. And what do I find, when I finally cash in my chips? A fucking petri dish! Sinister seams of dirt glint at me from the nooks and crevices of my complicated, mechanical bed. Whenever I shift to plump a pillow or pour myself a glass of water, I can feel pieces of grit trapped in my bedclothes, like soil lurking in the folds of a leek. In the ward lavatory, grey sludge coagulates on the funnels of the liquid-soap dispensers.

I am not one to leap to paranoid conclusions – particularly ones that involve God – but I have to admit that during my stay here the thought that I might be receiving some sort of divine retribution has crossed my mind once or twice. Hospital itself – the wretched communality of it, the enforced proximity of other people's leaking, cratered bodies, the yellow shafts of sunlight clogged with floating particles of sick people's skin – would have been trial enough for me. (I am a man who has spent his entire adult life squatting, tremblingly, a few inches above lavatory seats, just to avoid resting on other men's arse-prints; I don't even like to touch a door handle in a public bathroom for fear of all those crotchy hands that have grasped it before mine.) But that I should have ended up in a place like this – where patients trudge through the corridors with wafers of lavatory paper stuck to the soles of their slippers and even the nurses look as if they haven't changed their knickers in a while – seems too custom-made a nightmare to be the work of mere ill fortune.

Apart from my girlfriend Penny, and Art, I have received few visitors during my incarceration. A couple of friends have sent flowers. Some have even had hideous wicker cradles of 'Tele-fruit' delivered. But not one has seen fit to make an actual in-the-flesh appearance. My sister Monika offered to fly over from England in the first week, but I told her there was no need. My mother has called once to let me know that since I am a smoker she doesn't think it appropriate to extend sympathy for my current condition. My one extant daughter has made no contact whatsoever. Like her deceased sibling, she has refused to have anything to do with me for nearly a decade – a policy that has occasionally been relaxed in times of financial need, but is otherwise unbendable – even, it seems, by the news of my near-demise. Not that I mind. I am rather curious to know what she said when Monika told her I had had a heart attack. (My sister is far too discreet to volunteer that sort of information, and I don't want to look pathetic by asking.) But I have no desire for some kissy *rapprochement*. Oh God, no.

Sophie has always intimidated me. I was awkward around both of my daughters – embarrassed by their little pink bodies, appalled by their pukings and snottings, convinced that if they cuddled too close I would get an erection – but I was especially nervous of Sophie. She was, by anyone's standards, a daunting child – creepily self-possessed and knowing about adult matters. When she was four she asked me, with a dour little face, if I 'loved lots of ladies' or 'just Mummy'. Much later on, when she was found out doing unpleasant things at Margaret's, people blamed it on me – the traumas I had inflicted on her. But the truth is, Sophie's oddness predated all that and was entirely her own.

By the age of seven, she was talking about sex non-stop – not the giggly scatalogical references that one might have expected from a child of that age – but unsmiling, rather bleak observations on desire. 'You want to make love to her, don't you?' she once remarked to one of our dinner-party guests as he was eyeing a bosomy young woman across the table. 'You would like to roll and roll and roll in bed with her, wouldn't you?' We pretended to be amused by all this, Oona and I. We had an idea that we were both worldly people – that this little de Sade in knee socks who had sprung up in our midst was proof of what a broad-minded household we ran. 'What is that meant to be?' Oona would ask briskly when presented with one of Sophie's pornographic, kindergarten scrawls. (Oona always spoke to the children in the military, C.L.A.P. mode – Clear, Loudly, As an order, with Pauses.) 'A vagina? Well, it's a rather feeble vagina, darling. Where are the labia?' But we were not worldly people. Sex when we were growing up had been a vast, smutty enigma – an enigma whose depths we were still not entirely certain of having plumbed. Sophie frightened both of us.

Soon after she started secondary school, some classmates of Sophie's spray-painted the front garden wall of our house with the words, SOPHIE LIVES HERE. RING THE BELL. £5 A SCREW. Oona immediately called the school to complain. I made (empty) threats to go and find the boys and give them a good kicking. Sophie just giggled softly and wandered out of the living room, leaving us to rant. When I went to look for her a little later, I found her out in the street, calmly amending the graffito with a stick of chalk. She was adding two zeroes to the £5.

To occupy my arid hospital days, I have been watching a fair amount of television and sleeping a great deal. I have also been reading Sadie's journals. This was not my original intention. When I first got to hospital, I instructed Penny to get rid of them – wrap them up and send them on to Monika in London. Baby Pearl could be given the tchotchke when she was old enough, I thought. And as for the scrib-blings, Monika could do what she liked with them. I was furious, to tell the truth – repulsed by the whole manipulat-ive, TV mini-seriesness of the situation. If this was my daughter reaching out from the grave to mess with my conscience, I was having none of it.

But then, after Penny had gone off, I was stricken with doubt. Perhaps Sadie had included a message for me some-where in the legal pads. Perhaps she had even enclosed a letter. I had not inspected the package very carefully, after all. Such, presumably, were the sappy second thoughts that Sadie had been counting on. Old Willy might be a shit, but even he wouldn't be so bastardly as to just dismiss his daugh-ter's pre-suicidal wishes without some agonizing. In a panic of remorse, I rang Penny at my house and told her I wanted to see the journals once more before she sent them off.

She brought them in that night. There was no note, of course. I held up each pad in turn and shook it vigorously over my blanketed lap, but nothing fell out. Then I went to the last page of the third journal to see if it contained anything pertaining to Sadie's suicide. Again, there was nothing. Her final entry, a week before her death, was not remotely portentous – just an account of meeting an ex-boyfriend. Not exactly perky but not the sort of thing that suggests an imminent decision to do herself in.

Still, I did not hand the journals back to Penny. I told

her to come back and pick them up the next day. And then, when she dutifully returned the following afternoon, I put her off for another twenty-four hours. This went on for two or three days until I had to acknowledge that I was keeping the journals. I had begun reading them, you see – staying up until one or two in the morning and waking again at five, specifically to plough through my daughter's splodgy, felt-tip hieroglyphs.

At first, my progress was very slow. I found that I was unable to look at the journal for much more than ten minutes at a time without getting pissed off and developing pains in my gut – terrible, fluttery pains, like the first, prophetic murmurings of a bad clam. But I have slowly grown more resilient. At this point, I am able to read for quite long stretches without so much as a wince. I have even stopped humming loudly when I get to particularly uncomfortable passages.

The early stuff is not without historical interest. I am disinterring all sorts of long-forgotten details about my life, and, of course, I am also remembering Sadie. At ten, she was still basically a boy – a slight, skinny thing with an odd, froggy sort of face and many whimsical rituals: folding all her clothes, from her knickers to her hairband, into geometric patterns on a chair before she went to bed at night; going to sleep with her arms folded piously across her chest, like the girls in *Little House on the Prairie*. In the afternoons, after school, she used to play for hours at something called 'french skipping' – leaping in and out of two parallel lengths of elastic tied around chair-legs and singing a strange song about a daddy who bought a donkey. 'Donkey died, daddy cried. Inky pinky ponky.' She had a crush on Elvis. She was against putting pepper in scrambled eggs on the grounds that it looked like bugs eating daisies. She had a tortoise who fell into the garden pond and drowned. Amazingly, she loved me.

2

3 March 1971

Dad is notorious now because noone can find him. he has been in all the news papers. We are not supposed to read them incase we get upset but we had a look in the sweetshop next to school. Sophie says they all think dad killed mum because otherwise why would he run away and not face the music. Sophie agrees with them but thats not fair because the newspapers arent objective. We are staying with Aunt Monika and Morty who is her boyfriend from America. Aunt Monika lives in Queensgate. her flat has furry wallpaper which is called flok. we are meant to go to school on the tube but yesterday morty gave us money for a taxi. Morty and monika are living in sin even though they are quite old because Monika does not believe in marriage. She says she feels terrible for us and we are poor migts. but it is quiet trying for her because she has never had children and is not used to them and also she is not that young anymore and we are a handful. morty lets us drink chocolate nesquick because the milk is good for us and today after school he brought me a brill set of karen dash pencils. they were meant to be for sophie too but she is really too old for them. Today at school, Tracy Letts said I couldn't join in kisschase because my dad is a criminal and when the playground lady heard her she told her off. sophie said she was just jealous because our life is so glamorous!!!

I am clean. Nearly. One of the nurses came in at around four today and announced that she was taking me for a bath. The Bev Mem is evidently running some kind of Ugly Only hiring policy. This creature, whose name tag identified her as Dionne, had a tide mark around her neck and a greyish mole on her left cheek, sprouting two long, reedy hairs – like a cartoon desert island. Shortly after she had delivered her exciting news, another nurse, called Caresse, with greasy hair and udder-like breasts, arrived. (One nurse is generally considered sufficient to preside over the bathing process, but I got special dispensation, presumably on account of my unusual stroppiness.) The two women set about heaving me from my bed and into a wheelchair, and when this operation was complete they wheeled me out to the elevator and up three floors to a bathroom. Here, they presented me with a bath they had prepared earlier: a few inches of pale green tepid water in a plastic tub. I counted three hairs – very possibly pubic – floating in it.

'You have to be joking,' I said.

Dionne and Caresse looked at me blankly.

'Girls . . .' I pleaded.

'Come on, Mr Muller,' Dionne said, goggling at me hotly. 'We're not putting up with any tantrums.'

'But I asked for a bath, not a filthy fucking puddle!' I yelled.

Dionne and Caresse looked at one another. 'Mr Muller, I'm not having you curse at me,' Dionne said. She leaned down as she said this and I caught a gust of her hot, horsey breath. 'We've run this bath now,' she went on, 'and we don't waste water in this hospital. Get. In. The bath.'

She started pulling me up from the wheelchair.

'What?' I said. 'In front of you?' It hadn't really occurred to me that I was going to have to expose myself to these women. (Does a man become more keenly protective of his dignity in middle age? Or is it just that middle age opens up so many fresh opportunities for folly and humiliation?)

Dionne rolled her eyes. 'Don't worry, Mr Muller, you haven't got anything we haven't seen before.'

This is it, I told myself as I clambered, trembling with rage, into the brackish shallows of the tub – *this is what I have become. A naked old fool, bullied by foul-smelling slatterns called Dionne.*

I remember reading a phrase in a book once about a man being 'too poor to die'. It referred to a Victorian gentleman, fallen on hard times, who was about to expire without sufficient funds to pay his death duties or furnish a proper funeral. I am not that far gone. Dying, I could just about cover. It's just the rest of my lousy, invalid life that I can't afford. Dying, I tell myself sometimes, in a sudden, internal explosion of misery, would probably be my most sensible option right now. Certainly the thrifty thing to do. I wouldn't have to pay my impossibly high health-insurance premiums. I wouldn't have to write the shitty life story of Reginald Shitty Boon. I wouldn't have to die straight away either. I could afford a couple of weeks of comfortable fading – get in some good whiskey, a few cartons of Gauloises – live it up a little and then drop dead. Dying would be a bargain. A snip. I have never been all that wedded to the idea of life, anyway. God knows, beneath the mandatory pretence of treasuring every sunrise and so on, everyone is secretly day-dreaming of cancer and car accidents, aren't they?

But I won't kill myself, of course. There's the maddening thing. If you haven't done it by the time you get to my age, it's a fair bet you don't have the balls. The nearest I ever got was when I jumped bail before the first trial. I was very frightened. The case was getting a lot of press – all of it hostile to me – and I began to realize that I really might end up in prison. A surprising number of people base their ideas about the penal system on sitcoms. They think prison is a lot of cosy old duffers in jumpsuits arguing over the baccy ration. But I knew better. I had done a report on British prison conditions three years before, for 24/7. I had interviewed 'Derek', a glassy-eyed former inmate, who had been ritually pissed on and burned with cigarettes throughout his five years in Reading. Derek hadn't been a child-abuser or a wife-beater – just an embezzling account-ant whom the other prisoners and the guards hadn't taken to. Lovely.

So I ran. My friend Harry Ferguson gave me the keys to his place in Cornwall. I think he fancied the idea of being a crucial player in some sexy international crime episode. The plan, I am embarrassed to recall now, was that I would befriend a Cornish fisherman and have him take me on his boat to France or the Scillies. There I would wait, while Harry arranged a fake passport and a new identity for me.

What fantasies we are willing to entertain when we are truly desperate. The 'contacts' of whom Harry had boasted turned out to be a bunch of sandwich-shop robbers. The only thing they'd ever forged were Barbra Streisand concert tickets. As for the idea of me 'befriending' some surly Cornish sea-dog – well, let's just say it was never a very likely scenario. In the end I just sat in the cottage, freezing my tits off, eating pigeons from Harry's freezer and watching stories about myself on the news, until the police came and got me. It was during this period that I entertained what the shrinks call suicidal ideation. The ideation bit was a piece of cake. I just never could summon up the gumption to go ahead and do it. Interesting, that. What did Sadie have in her that I didn't?

By the time I got back to bed from my bath, dinner had been brought. One of the many barbarisms they insist on here is that all meals are served at least three hours before you would possibly want them. Thus breakfast turns up at 6.30, lunch at 11.45. A gruesome 'snack' appears on the stroke of 2.30 and the evening meal (on a little cling-wrapped tray) rolls around at 5 p.m. I have grown pretty stoic about the food here, but tonight, the culinary offerings – a beige slab of chicken on a sludgy bed of salad; a baked potato with a tub of a butter-flavoured, non-animal-fat spread called 'Buttery'; a bowl of fruit salad consisting mainly of bruised apple chunks and mauve-tinted grapefruit segments – were too upsetting. I poked at the reptilian skin of my baked potato for a while and then I gave up. At around seven, my phone rang.

'Willy!' my mother shrieked. 'Willy! Is that you?'

My mother left Germany for England over forty years ago, but she still speaks like a stormtrooper.

'Yes, Herr Kommandant, this is Willy.'

'What did you call me?'

'I called you Herr Kommandant.'

'I can't be long, the phone is too expensive. I just wanted to tell you that you must start eating soy bean protein immediately. It's excellent for heart problems. Willy?'

'I'm here.'

'Yes, so, a little soy bean protein – it's called tofu. Every day you should be eating this. You can buy it in a health shop.'

'Okay, *Mutti*. That's very nice of you. How are you doing?'

'No, Willy, I can't afford this tittling-tattling. You'll remember the tofu, *ja*?'

'Yes I will. Thank . . .'

'Your health problems are taking years off my life.'

'I'm sorry to hear that . . .' I began. But the phone had gone dead.

My mother feels very strongly that her entire existence has been spent taking the fall for the venality and malfeasance of others. First it was my father, Hermann, who committed the double error of being a Jew and a professor of political philosophy in 1930s Germany. (He made her flee to Spain in 1936 and then, pretty much as soon as they arrived, dropped dead with heart failure.) Then Monika and I inherited the burden of ruining her life. She went back to Germany for a short time after my father died, but our demi-Jewishness forced her out again, to miserable exile in England. Finally, when she thought nothing more could go wrong, I, her idiot son, brought a vulgar crime scandal to her door.

I tried reading more of Sadie's journal after my mother had rung off, but I soon threw it down in a fit of irritation. What idiocy this was, to be mooning over my dead daughter's drivel! With trembling hands, I tried to tear the pad in two. When I failed, I threw it on the floor, where it has been lying ever since.

3

4 April 1971

Dear Diary,
Aunt Monika said she couldnt cope with us and so now
we are living in Leeds with aunt Margaret and uncle Bill.
Margaret helps people who are sad and also she makes
art out of broken glass and other things that people dont
normally see the beauty in.

  Uncle bill is an artist too but he is also a plumber to
make ends meet. Now I have a new therapist called
doctor brock. His hair is died and he might be a poof. I
see doctor Brock twice a week. He says sophie and me
have had to grow up very fast. I like him, even though he
is a bit soppy, but Sophie thinks he is a wally because he
asked her if Dad ever tried to be intimate with her and
that is so sick. He asked me that too, but I didnt care
because he has to know these matters or he woudnt be
doing his job. sophie says it's immoral to miss dad
because what about mum? We are going to go to a new
school but first we are going to get some new clothes
because Aunt Margaret says the clothes we brought are
not practical. It can be abit boring here because there are
no good shops and they dont know much about fashion
in Leeds. Sophie says it is a dump. Last week she made
a penis out of plasticine and put her mouth on it. She
said that is what boys like. It looked DISGUSTING.
she has been cutting up rough and getting on everyones
nerves including mine!!!! Joshua, James and Ruth are
quiet nice but quiet square. they make jewellery out of

macaroni and their hobbies are reading maps and papiay mashay.

I am getting out tomorrow. Penny was in this morning – allegedly to help get me organized – but mainly, it seems, to harass and annoy me. 'Please, baby,' she cooed, whenever I swore at her. 'Don't be cussing Jesus.' My girlfriend spent the first seventeen years of her life as a Mormon in Provo, Utah. She ran away after that and her life has been studiously ungodly ever since, but her unfortunate beginnings still make themselves felt from time to time in these arbitrary bursts of pious twee. I kept pretending to drift off, but she didn't take the hint, and whenever I opened my eyes I would find her leaning over me – her face about an inch from mine.

Penny is a bit bizarre-looking at that proximity. Bodily speaking, she is quite appealing. She has good, big breasts (artful saline implants) and long legs, with tantalizing, unliposuckable pads of fat at the very top of the inner thighs. But her face is always a minor shock for the first moment or so. The eyelids are laden with some sort of grey shine that tends to work its way into her wrinkles over the course of the day, creating a series of oily grey circumflexes. The eyelashes are glued together into solid black blocks that make a little *pat* noise when they hit her cheeks. The lips are brown and glossy, like varnished wood. Two nose surgeries have left her nostrils pinched and undersized – like the little black dots on a dolly-proboscis. And thanks to a series of laser treatments, together with one drastic face lift performed by a hack surgeon she tried to sue, she wears a perpetual expression of parched exhilaration. Penny has worked as a make-up artist for most of her adult life, which perhaps explains the oddly provisional status she accords her physical self. At forty-whatever-she-is, she is a palimpsest of surgical enhancements. Most recently, she has had Botox – a derivative of the botulism virus – injected into her forehead, to paralyse her brow and disable unsightly frown-lines. Now, when she is worried or concerned, the attempt to corrugate her forehead results in a weird, roiling motion beneath the skin.

'Poor baby,' she kept saying to me this morning, 'you not feeling good?'

'No,' I shouted finally, rearing up in my bed. 'I am not feeling good. Why would I be? I've got a terrible crick in my neck, and it smells like a leper colony round here . . .'

'Hey. *Hey*,' she interrupted. 'Cool down, mister. You know something? You got to concentrate on getting better, d'ya hear?'

At this, I collapsed back on to my pillows. I am fond of Penny. I really am. She is one of the kindest stupid women I have ever known. But sometimes the monotony of her dumbness is more than I can bear. She claims to have been educated somewhere, but she is, at best, semi-literate. Her handwriting is the kind you see on the blackboard menus in transport cafés – lower case and capitals all mixed up. And she speaks as if she had learned English from watching soap operas. 'You know something, Willy?' she'll say. 'You can't run away from you.' Or, 'Know something?' – always that grim locution – 'you can't count your blessings in the dark.' Or, 'Know something? – you can't take care of anyone else till you take care of yourself.' For some reason, this last one particularly grates on me. It reminds me of the instructions you receive on aeroplanes telling you, in the case of an emergency, to put on your own oxygen mask first, before attending to the child you are travelling with. I haven't gone anywhere in the company of children for many years, but the image of some infant turning blue and expiring as I faff ineptly with my plastic tubes still makes me horribly anxious.

Much as Penny's fortune-cookie wisdoms irk me, I often

find myself feeding her the cues for them. I guess I must find them comforting in some way. For instance, at a certain point this morning I asked her to get me a cigarette. 'Penny, go get me a cigarette would you?' I said, even though I had not the slightest expectation that she would. Sure enough, she sighed and stroked my head and said, 'Hey, big guy. *Hey*. You know something? You gotta forget about the cigarettes.'

I have a long, baroque history of trying to forget about cigarettes. I've done it all – herbal cigarettes, nicotine gum, nicotine patches, children's pacifiers. I've paid fantastic sums for inspirational encounter sessions with stop-smoking gurus. I've been hypnotized. I've had needles stuck in me. At some point in the mid seventies I even hired an aversion therapist to come round to my house three times a week and administer electric shocks to my wrists while I chain-smoked in front of a mirror. (After a fortnight I was forced to concede that I was getting to quite like the shocks.) Most recently, I went to the famous Nosmo King Camp in the Arizona desert, where campers are required to perform group exercises and wear tee-shirts that say, 'I'm a quitter . . . and I'm proud of it!' On the third day of my visit I was spotted by one of the camp guides, zooming out of the Nosmo grounds at ninety miles an hour. A rather mortifying chase ensued and I was finally cornered in the parking lot of a shimmering desert mall, furiously scrabbling at the cellophane wrapping on a just-purchased carton of Lucky Strikes. This episode alone would not have been sufficient to exhaust the good will of the Nosmo King authorities. But the next day I told a female camper who wanted me to be her partner in a cactus-decoration competition to fuck off. That pretty much broke the Nosmo camel's back. I was the first inmate in the camp's history to be asked to leave.

'Listen,' Penny said. 'I saw Art yesterday. He wants to

come see you tomorrow when you get out. He told me to give you this.' She handed over an airmail envelope with what appeared to be several Polaroid photographs inside. I put the envelope on the bedside table to open after Penny left. Art is in the habit of sending me dirty pictures. I once had a cleaning lady tender her resignation after she came across a set of nineteenth-century rotogravures that Art had sent me for my birthday depicting a solemn Victorian gentlewoman in various states of sexual congress with an equally solemn Victorian horse. Although I am not particularly interested in pornography myself, I enjoy Art's innocent, old-world enthusiasm for naked ladies. I find it oddly touching. Art has never gotten over his initial amazement upon discovering that there were women in the world prepared to do lewd things in front of cameras for money.

'Aren't you going to open it?' Penny asked, looking at the envelope. I grunted a negative.

Penny cocked her head. 'Go on. They're photographs.'

'Uh-huh,' I said.

'I know what they're of.' Her voice took on an infuriating sing-song. I was silent.

'Oh, Willy, don't be mean!' Penny exclaimed. 'Don't you want to know? They're of this place that Art wants us to go stay at while you're convalescing.'

I still didn't open the envelope. It irritated me that Penny had known what was in it before I did. It irritated me that I was irritated. *What a petty-minded little fuck I am,* I thought. I wished Penny would leave.

'It's in Mexico,' Penny went on. 'It's meant to be really beautiful . . .'

'Oh, *super*,' I said, nastily. 'Just what I need. Quesa-fucking-dillas. What is this? A plot to kill me?'

Penny looked at me with an expression of cute reproach. 'Hey, you. Art says it's a really neat place.'

I shut my eyes. I really thought I might expire with irritation. 'I have to sleep.'

'Okay, baby.' Penny said. 'I guess I'll go, then.' She bent over and kissed me on the lips. I could smell the pukey, cinnamon smell of her sugar-free gum. 'See you tomorrow. Take care.' She paused. 'Sleep well.' Another, longer pause. I could sense that she was still there, poised over me like a lovelorn tarantula. 'Okay. Goodbye, baby,' she said. 'Love ya . . . Goodbyeee . . .' And when I finally opened my eyes again, she was gone.

4

28 May 1971

*Dad will be in prison for years and years. aunt margaret
cried when she told us but sophie said that is because she
is sad for mum. sophie hates him now. but me and aunt
monika still love him and the whole story has not been
told. Some reporters came to the house on friday but
uncle bill talked to them and we weren't allowed to go
outside. when he came in again he said they are just
locus. he gave me an extra piece of fruit and nut after
dinner. sophie had a sex romp with rob and joshua and
ruth on saturday in the garage and aunt margaret has
found out about it all because ruth said golden rain at
dinner. I wasn't allowed in because sophie said I had to
stand guard outside so I am not in as much trouble. aunt
margaret has made rob and joshua and ruth tell
everything and now she is super furious. she says sophie
is unspeakable and she is at her witsend. But Sophie says
she was only educating them and that Auntie Margaret
ought to be grateful. Aunt Margaret called Monika but
Monika said she can't be expected to have us back
because sophie could give Morty a stroke. Everything is
quiet horrible at the moment.*

Today I left hospital. Penny drove me home. Sitting weakly
in the passenger seat of her BMW, I gazed out of the
window at West Los Angeles whizzing by. The sun on the
buildings was hard and white, and the people I glimpsed
in other cars seemed to be clutching their steering wheels

very tightly. When Penny pulled up at a set of traffic lights on Beverly Boulevard, I thought I saw a woman I've slept with a couple of times driving a brand new, bright red convertible. I slid down in my seat, to avoid being seen, but when the lights changed and I peeped through the window, I saw that it was not her after all – just someone with a similar shade of auburn hair. She had a vanity registration plate on her car that spelt, 'Heh Heh'.

Nine years ago, when I first came to Los Angeles, I really believed I had found my perfect city. It was a golden time, that first month, padding about the fusty suite of my cheap hotel, looking like a Weimar industrialist in my fat bathrobe; dabbing off drips of maple syrup from my sun-baked belly as I took breakfast by the pool; watching a woman in a yellow G-string prepare to dive, the words PROPERTY OF MIKEY tattooed just above her bikini line. I'd been in *prison*, for God's sake. LA seemed to me a place of limitless erotic promise – gleaming, hygienic days, mysterious, noirish nights. Everything about it spoke of sex: the galloping freeways; the roaring Niagara of my hotel shower; the odd, swimming-pool fragrance of the tap-water; the ticklish shiver and momentary blindness that occurred whenever I passed from a sunny street into the dark cool of an air-conditioned lobby.

I'm not sure exactly when all these things ceased, or when they ceased to excite me. I guess it's been a slow ebb. There are too many cars now, and you have to travel an hour up the coast just to find a stretch of water that isn't bobbing with human shit. Mostly, these days, LA makes me feel anxious. Anxious and bored – one of life's least desirable combinations.

Sometimes I think about moving, but the thoughts never get very far. Where am I going to go? London is out of the question. Miami revolts me. Manhattan, whatever anyone says, is an arsehole of a town. Oona and I spent one of our wedding anniversaries there. (Her parents paid.) She enjoyed the way grocery stores sold Brussels sprouts in punnets as if they were something special, like raspberries. And she was very taken with the glamorous bolshiness of the people. But the place was undeniably a dump. One morning, we stepped out of a coffee shop to see a tramp standing on a pedestrian island in the middle of Broadway whacking at the head of another tramp with a hammer. No thank you very much.

'Let's stop somewhere for lunch,' I said suddenly, as Penny made a left on to Wilshire.

Penny shook her head. 'I don't think that's such a good idea, babe.'

'I want to stop for lunch,' I said. 'Let's go to the Carnegie.'

She looked at me. 'You sure? Wouldn't you like to get home and rest? I could bring you some take-out . . .'

'Just take me to the deli,' I said.

Jesus, I'm such a prick to that woman.

The Carnegie was busy. As Penny pushed open the door, the noise of jabbering patrons came at us in a great gust. Penny and I were seated by the hostess at a booth towards the back of the restaurant. The previous customer had left behind that day's edition of *Variety*, which I immediately picked up and began to hungrily examine. Reading the trades, particularly if, like me, you are on the pathetic, envious periphery of the trade, is a bit like doing cocaine – you know you shouldn't; you know you always regret it later. But if the temptation presents itself, there is no question but that you will succumb.

Within seconds of picking up the paper, I spotted a smallish item on the bottom left of the front page announcing that Robert Siskowitz had just signed with Hercules Films to write the prequel to *Tiger Time* – the surprise kiddy smash of last year. Unbelievable. I knew Siskowitz years ago, when I was first in LA. Back then, he was writing the scripts for this TV programme called *Injury!* that reconstructed a different real-life accident every week. On a Monday, the producer would give Bob the research material on a particular disaster, and by Thursday he would have to present a thirty-minute script based on the car-crash or shark attack or whatever. The show ran in the very early hours of Sunday morning, and there were quite a few Saturday nights when a bunch of us guys wound up at Siskowitz's stinky West Hollywood apartment getting stoned and watching the show. Siskowitz was a big pot-head back then – still is, for all I know. He was an amiable enough guy, but I don't think anyone thought he was ever going to be anything but a loser. Then two years ago he sold Hercules this stupid little treatment for a kids' movie. About a family of *tigers*, for fuck's sake. The next thing you know, the movie is the biggest family hit since *E.T.* and Siskowitz is checking out the real estate in Malibu Colony. The item in *Variety* was headlined, BOB'S CATS PURR ALL THE WAY TO THE BANK. Tuh.

'Don't you want to look at the menu?' Penny asked.

'I know what I want,' I said, without looking up. 'I'm having a pastrami on rye.'

Penny's eyes widened. 'Lookit, mister! No way! Pastrami is about the worst thing you could eat right now. Why don't you try the fruit salad? That's what I'm having.'

Penny is genuinely baffling to me. She has been with me on and off for five years, and in that time I have refused to let her leave a single item of clothing, or even a toothbrush, at my house. I can't have visited her more than twice in her own apartment – a dingy little place she shares with a girlfriend over in West Hollywood. Another woman might have grown discouraged. But not Penny. She sticks to me, like a limpet to a rock. She will acknowledge that we have our problems, but she is confident that we are making progress. One of these days, she says, I will resolve my personal-space issues. Her stoicism would be understandable if I had money, or charm, or an enormous penis. But I have none of these things. It's odd.

She is not helpless. This is a woman who ran away from the Mormons at seventeen, after all. (Her daddy was mean to her, she once told me. Plus she was curious to know what Coca-Cola tasted like.) There are inner reserves of gumption there, I think – she is just disinclined to draw upon them in the normal run of things. A couple of times, over the years, I have caught snatches of Penny in off-duty mode. I've happened upon her talking to a store clerk, or a woman in the line at the bank – and in those instances, unburdened of the obligation to please, she seems quite foreign and mysterious – another woman entirely. Her whole body sags as if it has been released from a corset. Her voice loses its helium squeal and descends an octave or two to relative normality. Her face darkens and closes. At such moments I confront the shocking possibility that she is the owner of a private sensibility – that she has ideas and feelings that are not immediately accessible to me. But the impression never lasts more than a split second. The next moment, becoming aware of my gaze, she will realign herself and assume once again her mask of gormless candour.

When we got back home, I was desperate to be alone, but Penny insisted on coming in and making sure I was settled. My house is one of those rather wan 1950s bungalows that pepper the no-man's-land stretch of the Pacific Coast Highway after Santa Monica and before Malibu. Once inside it, you are sandwiched between the roar of the Pacific and the ceaseless wee-ow of the road. When I first came to Los Angeles, flush with the proceeds of *To Have and to Hold*, this shagpiled split-level on the sea, with a grotto fireplace and textured Paisley wallpaper, was about as close to real-estate heaven as I could think of without passing out in ecstasy. But these days it has a troubling, mothball scent about it – a general ambience of defeat. It is waiting, I think, for a new owner – someone rich and savvy to come along and tear it down, so that it can be reborn as a neo-Tuscan villa or a post-modern glass-house.

After pacing about in a gloomy, purposeless way, I went into my study and hooked up my lap-top, with the intention of putting in a good half hour on the Reggie Boon opus. Before I got into the ghosting business, I wrote a couple of unauthorized biographies – one about a British duke, the other about a Saudi prince. Both were composed in the popular-modern style – sycophantic, slyly impertinent, with mock-reluctant emphasis on their subjects' recondite sexual proclivities and 'battles with weight'. Both did pretty well. But eventually, on the advice of Art, I gave up the biography work and succumbed to ghosting, which requires less labour and is paid much better. It was Art who pointed out that as the infamous protagonist of an English manslaughter trial, I was a far more eligible amanuensis to the stars than I could ever have hoped to have been as a respectable journalist. I had established a foothold on the lower rungs of celebrity aristocracy – gone over to the other side. Now that the media had shat on *me*, showbusiness was happy to embrace me as one of its own.

Over the years, I have ghosted four autobiographies (one daytime soap-opera star, two talk-show hosts and a TV magician). I am a very good ghost, as it happens. I get on well with the subjects, who are usually rather flattered to have an Englishman with a passably posh voice documenting their favourite foods and most embarrassing moments. And I have a genuine talent for the language of what the publishing industry knows as 'sleb bio'. Since

there is no job so menial or frivolous that a skilled prac-
titioner cannot derive pleasure from doing it well, I find
my ghost work quite satisfying. For a moment in my study,
as the computer sounded its tinny fanfare, I found myself
actually eager to tackle the Reggie files.

But only for a moment. By the time I fished out the vast
sheaf of transcribed Boon interviews, inserted a clean disk,
pointed and clicked, I felt swoony with exhaustion. I sat
sifting through the transcript, reading snatches of Reggie's
maundering.

*Is it on? Right, okay. So, I can just start now, then? Okay
. . . (inaudible) . . . I was born on the 2nd of July, 1928,
just missed being a Yankee Doodle baby by two days. I
was the middle child of five. Sharon? Can you bring me a
Coke? Willy, you want a Coke? No? (inaudible) Okay
just make it one. There was my eldest sister Lucy, then
Elizabeth, then me. And after me came Irving and
Katharine. Funnily enough for a guy that grew up to be
so pug-ugly, I was a pretty cute baby. Being the first boy
to come along, I was spoiled rotten, too. Oh, great, just
put it there. Thanks, baby . . .*

I started flicking forward. Most of my interviews with
Boon, including this one, took place at his home in Bel Air.
Boon lives in a proper, old-fashioned Hollywood mansion,
with hollow pillars and uniformed servants and a pink-
bottomed, kidney-shaped pool. For all our sessions, we sat
in his rather depressing 'games room', a windowless cavern
at the bottom of the house with red quilted Naugehyde
walls and a pool table. (Boon loathes the sun. Forty years
on the west coast have left him with the blue-white pallor
of skimmed milk.) The games room is where all the framed
photographs of Boon yukking it up with celebrity golf
partners are kept. It also houses a South Sea Island-style

wet bar, although this, as far as I can tell, functions only as a tease. In the ten or fifteen times I went over there, the strongest thing Boon ever offered me was a tomato juice.

One day, I walked into the MGM refectory with my manager and I saw Morty Savitch sitting at one of the tables with a beautiful girl. I said to Johnny, 'Johnny, that's the girl I'm going to marry.' Swear to God. Of course, Johnny looks at me like I'm crazy – here's this beautiful broad having lunch with one of the most powerful men in the industry and there's me – this funny-looking little guy with a couple of bit parts to his name. So he looks at me and I says to him, 'You can look at me that way Johnny, but I'm telling you now, one day Reggie Boon is gonna be a star and that girl's gonna be his wife.' I was such a dumb innocent kid, it never occurred to me that Savitch was balling her . . .

I kept flicking.

I don't want to speak badly of Johnny – but to speak the truth, the man fucked me. You're gonna put something else in for fucked, right? I rang him at his house that night and I says, 'Johnny, you sonofabitch, you sold me down the river. I'm leaving you.' He pleads with me – he even gets Rose on the phone, asking me to forgive him. That was Johnny – cheesy to the last bite. But I don't budge. 'Sorry Johnny,' I says, 'but that's the way it is.' You can say a lot of things about Reggie Boon, but when his mind is made up, that's it. There ain't heaven or hell gonna move him from his point of view . . .

I put the manuscript down and started to pace about the room. Then I sat down on a sofa and rummaged in my suitcase for the photographs that Penny had brought me from Art. The pictures, which I had already examined several times, were of a two-storey Spanish-style villa, with a red-tile roof and two large verandas. In almost all of them, a skinny, deeply tanned woman with a sharp face and knees like gnarled apples stood in a bikini, making goofy gestures. This was apparently the owner of the property and the author, no doubt, of the cute comments written on the back of the prints:

Still crazy after all these years!

Another beautiful sunset

You don't have to be mad to work here, but it helps!

'*The Casa De La Luna gang*' (This, for a shot of the woman standing with her arms around a young Mexican man in white uniform, and a crinkle-faced Mexican hag in a black dress and white apron.)

I stared at the woman's wizened, cognac-coloured belly. Art's life is a vast tangle of favours owed and owing. He was no doubt getting a discount on a gross of bath towels, or a job for one of his nephews, in exchange for finding this witch a summer tenant. Whatever the deal was, I knew I would never get to the bottom of it. I would be made to feel honour-bound to help Art out – to rent the villa at some exorbitant price for the sake of my old pal who was in a fix too complex to be specified. Then, when I had been harried into saying yes, I would find myself indebted for having been given a deal on such a desirable holiday residence.

When Art turned up later on, he was in a bad, indigestion-related mood which he insisted on dressing up in a sort of hostile good cheer.

'Willy, you smelly old cripple!' he shouted when he arrived. 'You look like shit! Ha! Ha! Ha!' He was breathing heavily, and as he moved I could see his flesh jiggling beneath his tent-like silk suit. Why the hell didn't *he* have the heart attack?

He took my head between his two big, pink hands and planted a noisy kiss on my brow. I smiled fraily and gave a papal nod. Art is big on kissing and cuddling. It is one of the things – along with his fatness and the vats of Eau Sauvage that he pours over his immense body – that dates him. He doesn't understand the *froideur* of the new young agents and studio executives – the men with Ivy League degrees and thick, lustrous hair who flinch when he tries to paw them. 'We Jews are warm people!' he admonishes them. Even I – who hate to be touched intimately by men – learned long ago to submit quietly to Art's embraces.

Art grew up in Bensonhurst, Brooklyn, the son of a herring merchant. He trained as a lawyer in the fifties, and his first job when he came out to California was doing contracts for the late, legendary theatrical agent Sonny Green. (I have no idea if Green is really legendary – that's just what people always say about him. His legendariness is legendary even if he isn't.) Art has been running his own little agency out of a three-room office in Beverly Hills for almost twenty-five years now. For the last ten of them, he has been haemorrhaging all his better clients to the big-boy agencies. He is too smart not to know that his end is nigh, but every time another one of his snot-nosed little actors or 'writer-directors' walks out on him, he is wounded afresh. 'Cock*sucker*,' he'll murmur in wonderment. 'Treated the boy like a son . . . Cock*sucker*.'

We were out on the deck. Art waved away the offer of a chair and stood with his back to the sea, sucking nervously on the great jelly-bean gemstone of his pinky ring. I was laid out on a recliner, with a plaid blanket folded across my lap. ('Take the fucking thing away,' I had told Penny, when she had brought it out for me earlier. But Penny is in some delirium of nursely virtue that no unpleasantness can penetrate. She just ignored me and whisked off, smiling.)

She came out on the deck now, with a tray of iced tea for us.

'So,' Art said, turning to her, 'how is the patient? Has he had his way with you yet?'

Penny giggled. 'Oh, *Art*!' she crowed, gleefully.

'Come on!' Art bellowed, warming to his smut. 'You mean you two young lovebirds haven't fucked yet? Whassa-madda, Willy? You big mo! Scared your heart can't take it? Put her on top, for Chrissakes!' He laughed – a terrible gargling, as if a small animal were being drowned in saliva at the back of his throat.

'Oh, Art!' Penny said again.

'No, but really, Willy,' Art continued, when Penny had gone back inside. He lowered his voice, to indicate impending sentiment. 'It's beautiful to see you looking better and back at home.' The late afternoon sky had grown wan and our hair was dancing crazily in the wind coming off the ocean. Both Art and I are balding, but Art is definitely suffering the more extreme and inelegant hair-loss. My hair is merely beginning to ebb at the temples. Art's scalp is a glowing pink dome, circumscribed by a tiara of dyed frizzle. ('It's called Mahogany,' he told me, the first time he presented the dye job. 'In this business, Willy, grey is for sofas.') Now, as I observed Art's pink and orange head, I felt my spirits lift slightly.

'I've got to tell you, you had me scared there for a little while,' Art went on. 'I don't think I could have taken it if you hadn't pulled through. Honest to God.'

I smiled. 'Art,' I said. 'I'm not going to Mexico.'

Art drew himself upright, throwing his shoulders back and his chest forward. His affronted posture. 'Hello?' he shouted. 'Come again? Did I miss out on something here or was I just trying to tell you I loved you?'

'Yes, you were,' I said, 'and I appreciate it. But I just wanted to tell you, I took a look at your pictures of Casa

37

De La Gringo and I have no intention of stepping foot in the place.'

'Fuck you!' Art roared. 'Fuck you! You think this is all about you?'

'Well,' I said, pretending not to be cowed, 'in this particular instance, yes.'

Art paused. 'Okay,' he said, rubbing his big, open-pored face with his hand. 'Okay. Here's what I think:' Art has a habit of framing his sentences like this. ('It's called contextualization,' he explained to me once, when I pointed it out to him. 'It lets a person know what the sentence is going to be about before they hear it. You know why I'm a good agent? You know why I can deal with those fucks at the studios better than anybody? Huh, Willy? Because I use *colons*.')

'Here's what I think:' Art said now. 'You're a very unwell guy.'

'I know,' I said. 'So how come you're shouting at me?'

'Honest to God,' Art said, 'you don't look good. You're tired right now and you don't feel like moving anywhere. But believe me, once you're out there, eating papaya and getting blown by the maid, you're gonna thank me for this. I'm a close personal friend of Sissy Yerxa, who owns the place. I can get you a great rate. Did you see the picture of the pool with the Renaissance mosaic on the bottom?'

'I saw it,' I said. 'I'm not going.'

'Okay,' Art said wearily. 'Do you want to take me through your decision tree on this?'

I shook my head. 'Don't start with me, Art. I've never liked Mexico. I don't like the heat. The place is full of bugs that want to crawl up your arse and give you incurable diseases. And what happens if I get sick? I don't want some Mexican doctor sticking his hands in my chest.'

Art immediately held up his hand and began to count off the points on his pudgy fingers. 'Okay. Heat: Pee Vee

38

at this time of year has, like, an ideal temperature. I mean, it's got the most temperate frigging climate in the world. You get cool sea breezes all day long and in the evening a light refreshing rain.'

'This Sissy Jerk-off must really have you over a barrel,' I said. 'What did you do, impregnate her daughter or something?'

Art closed his eyes. 'Okay, and then hygiene or whatever? Let me tell you, Willy, this is not a dirty place. You don't see a bug from one month to the next. You can eat your dinner out of the toilet bowl, it's so clean. There's a maid who polishes every fucking surface all day long, seven days a week . . .'

'Is that the same maid who's going to be blowing me?' I interrupted.

Art smiled. 'Sure. Now, as to the medical situation – Willy, you think I would send you some place without the proper medical resources? This is a premiere VIP resort. They got an American hospital there!'

'I don't want to go, Art . . .'

'Let me ask you this, Willy,' Art asked. 'How much work have you done on Reggie Boon lately?'

'What's it got to do with Mexico?'

'Hup! Come on.'

'I've got some pages. I've been in hospital, for Christ's sake. You can't expect any man to be prolific under those conditions.'

'Well, here's the thing, Willy. The people over at Hegley's are pissed. They're threatening to cancel the contract and take back the advance money.'

'Oh, Jesus . . .'

'I've staved them off for a little while, told them your daughter died . . . But I want you to forget about Reggie's project for a little while, anyway. The situation has changed.'

I wonder whether it is something unique to agents – this infuriating insistence on rationing out information in discrete, tantalizing parcels.

'What do you mean?'

'I spoke to Phil Buscemi the other day. Things are looking very good for *To Have*.'

'Uh-huh.' Buscemi is the executive at Curzon who is in charge of my screenplay.

'The studio is very excited about the picture. They've sent it to Hans Stempel . . .'

'Who?'

'Stempel. Hans. The guy who did *Das Warrior* . . .'

'A *Kraut*?'

'Oh, please. Yes, a German. He has a *lot* of juice right now.'

'I never heard of him.'

'Well, the last movie did nothing over here but everyone peed their pants about it at the European festivals. He's meant to be the leading exponent of meaningful action. Anyway, he loves the script. He's really interested.'

'So that's good, right? I should be happy, right?'

'Yeah! But he won't commit until he's got some changes . . .'

'What changes? Major stuff?'

'No, no, no. Minimal. You know, the usual shit, to make him feel like he's putting his imprint on the project.'

'He's going to direct the movie! What more of an imprint does he need?'

'Look, it's . . .'

'Am I going to get paid for rewrites?'

'Shut up a second, will you?'

'For Christ's sake, Art!'

'Will you shut up? You already managed to con the studio into buying an old script. You should be grateful . . .'

'*I* conned the studio?'

'This is very little work, and if Stempel says yes to directing this, it's a green-light project, no question. And Pee Vee is a great place to work.'

'Is a free rewrite in my contract?'

'No. But it doesn't look good if you start asking for more money now. I know it's a stretch for you, Willy, but you've got to act like a good sport.'

'Marvellous – now my agent is giving away my services for free . . .'

'Hup! Bup! Hold on a second there. I haven't finished yet. What do you think would happen if Buscemi or anyone over at Curzon knew you nearly died a couple of weeks back?'

'You mean you haven't told them?'

'Damn right, I haven't. They'd hire another writer immediately.'

'So, great. Another writer can work for nothing.'

'Yeah, another writer can share credit and take half your percentages on foreign and video. Work with me here.'

'So they don't know I've been sick at all?'

'Correct.'

'And whateverhernameis over at Hegley's – does she know?'

'Nope.'

'But she must have tried to call me. Buscemi must have tried to call me.'

'They would have, but the day you went into hospital, your genius agent rang and told them all you were in writer's retreat.'

'*Writer's retreat*? What the hell is that?'

'Don't get pissy with me!' Art bellowed. 'How the hell would I know? You're the writer. The point is, no one knows so far that you're sick. And no one will ever know, as long as you get out of town and don't stay here, dragging your heart-diseased carcass around.' He sucked on his pinky ring, expectantly.

'How soon do I need to get Boon done?'

'I told them you'd deliver by the end of the year.'

'And the rewrite?'

Art paused. 'Mid October. Listen, listen, listen. It's not so bad. Once you're out in Pee Vee, you gonna be turning out the pages like a fucking machine.'

I scowled at him. 'Stop calling it "Pee Vee", for Christ's sake.'

The ocean had turned very choppy now. A dog that had been leaping about in the rough surf, fetching a ball, lolloped up the beach and crouched a few yards away from my deck, to take a shit.

'Hey!' I shouted to the dog's owner, some tanned little guy in surfing shorts. 'Where do you get off letting your dog dump on the beach? You better be planning to pick that dogshit up.'

The man just looked at me – I could have been a piece of fruit or a sofa or something – and carried on walking. I stared after him. Then I turned back to Art. 'Okay,' I said, wearily, 'how much is this Mexican shithole going to cost me?'

5

20 September 1971

It is my birthday today and I am ten years old. I am now at Hazlitts School for Girls which is in Shropshire. On your birthday at Hazlitts, you get a special cooked breakfast and a birthday cake at tea-time. Dad sent me a card and it said when he comes out he will take me to any shop I choose and buy me anything I want. Sophie has gone to another school because she is a bad influence. I don't see a psychiatrist here. You can only use the telephone on the weekends. Dad says it is not really fair that I have to go to boarding school just because Sophie behaved badly but it is the cross I have to bear. He says one of these days he will come and take me out for a salt beef sandwich. He says we are in the same boat because we are both trying to get used to new instittuttions only the food is probably better where I am. The girls here are not as snobby as I thought they would be. some of them are quite cockney. My best friend so far is a girl called Liesl. she is a bit fat but has a lot of confidence. I am so ugly at the moment, I dont know what to do. My nose is becoming big like daddys and my hair is crap. also I have a lot of freckles. Aunt Margaret sent me a pottery ring which is horrible. Monika sent me a five pound book token. I have to play hockey here, which I have never played before and I must say it is quite a brutal and violent game.

After Art left, I went and lay down on my bed. When I woke, I had been dreaming freakish, pastel-coloured dreams of Mexico. I remained lying on the bed for a long time, listening to the ocean, watching the room grow black. I have been to Mexico twice in my life before now – once to attend a wedding in Mexico City, and once for a long weekend in Acapulco with a former Miss Ecuador called Christa. The first trip was horrendous. The air in Mexico City is three-dimensional with pollution. And the cockroaches! Vast, shiny brown things that stroll nonchalantly along the street, like ambulatory patent leather handbags. The whole place made me want to spend a recuperative month in the shower.

Acapulco was marginally more pleasant, but I still didn't really get the point. It was just America with poor hygiene. Christa had long blonde hair and a chain – a thin, thin, thread of gold – around her midriff. But I got the shits pretty much as soon as the plane touched down. For seventy-two hours I existed solely on a diet of codeine and black tea. And even then I had to clench my arse muscles during coitus in order to prevent myself from squittering.

Eventually I got up from bed and went into the living room. Penny was on the phone with a girlfriend.

'You need another therapist,' she was saying. 'You know something? You're a very special person . . .'

I stood there listening to her, growing gloomy. *What is the point of all this? What does Penny think the point is? Motivelessness, that's the issue. I'm without cause. And I am bad. A bad, bad, man. I have to be – because there's only that or being good, right? It's like when you see the news reports about men who go rushing into burning buildings to save their kids or whatever. And you think, okay, so that man's a hero – but what is the man who didn't rush in? Is he a coward? Because it seems like there should be more options on the moral menu. If doing the thing is so bloody extraordinary, then not doing it should just be considered regular. If those Poles who hid Jews in their haystacks were really such saints, why are the Poles who said to the Jews, fuck no, get out of here before you get me killed – why are they scoundrels?*

Penny caught sight of me now and waved.

Look at me, lurking by the door, thinking my amateurish philosophical thoughts. How can she bear it?

Filled with sudden pity for my girlfriend, I blew her a kiss.

6

26 December 1971

I got a lot of really brill prezzies for Xmas. Dad came to Monika and Mortys in the morning. we are spending our holidays there because theres not enough room in harrys flat for us. we ate smoked salmon and opened our presents. Dad ate a lot because he needs to put on weight and also he was dreaming of smoked salmon when he was in prison. He gave me a little record player in a black suitcase that I can carry with me and a record token for 10 pounds!!!! For lunch we went with monika and morty to claridges and morty paid. I had steak and chips and cornonthecob and Sophie had spaghetti and dad had chicken potpie. Morty and Monika had turkey because they wanted to be traditional. Dad is staying at harrys flat to write his book about mum. harry is away at his mums in the country so we went there and all lay on the sofa and watched The Wizard of Oz. In the evening, sophie and me got sad because mum was not there. sophie cried and I cried too but sophie said, really snotty, that I was just copying her, because I wanted some attention. we had a row and dad shouted at us to shut up! shut up! shut up! And then we cried even more.

I am dying, I thought this morning, coming awake suddenly in the soupy Mexican dawn. *I am dying – I should go back to Los Angeles.* Sunlight was filtering in through the shutter slats and the air was already heavy with heat. Next to me in my night-steamy bed, a woman called Karen lay on her front with her face smeared across the pillow. *Christ, this heat. Oh, what a broken-down old fuck I am. I am dying.*

Owing to a last-minute call for a job doing make-up on a commercial shoot in Arizona, Penny was unable to come out to Puerto Vallarta with me straight away. As a reflexive gesture, rather than in answer to any genuine desire, I arranged for Karen Spiceland to fill in during her absence. I ran into Karen last year at a party and we slept together once or twice after that. I'm not sure exactly how it ended – I assume I simply stopped calling her, but I can't be certain. Karen is young – not much more than twenty-five – tall and red-headed. She does something completely useless for one of the studios. She has blondish-pink eyebrows and she is diligently energetic in bed. This, when I called her three weeks ago, was the sum total of my recollections.

Since then, of course, my memory has been refreshed. On the plus side, Karen is rather more attractive than I had remembered. She is long and skinny to the point of gawkiness, with freckly legs and arms that flap about, uncertain of what to do with their noodly selves. She expends a great deal of breath when she talks – she pants, in fact, like someone who has walked up a very steep flight of stairs. This is one of those things that girls do on purpose to be sexy, and for some reason it is – even when you know it's a ploy. On the minus side, Karen is about as annoying as a human can be. Conversation-wise, she makes Penny look like George Sand.

Shortly after arriving in Puerto Vallarta, I realized that I would be unable to withstand much more than a week of Karen's undiluted company, so I started calling various friends in California, more or less begging to be visited. As a result, Richard Burnham and his girlfriend Heidi arrived from Los Angeles yesterday afternoon to stay for a week. Heidi is an executive at one of these new youth-music channels. She expresses approbation with the word 'cool' (pronounced with two syllables, to rhyme with 'jewel'). People often describe her as 'driven', which seems to function these days as the accepted euphemism for 'bitch'. Richard is a TV writer. Until a few years ago when he decided that some bum-fluffed Harvard jerk over at CAA, with a bunch of African art in his office, would better represent his interests, Richard was a client of Art's. We first met at Art's house, in fact. Art used to run a big Monday-night poker game and both Richard and I were regulars. Richard is a disagreeable poker player, tending to gloat sickeningly when he wins and throw hissy-fits when he loses. He is also one of the world's most dedicated freeloaders. But right now Richard is a prince to me, because he is going to save me from the nightmare that is life with Karen.

Women still want to have sex with me, I thought yesterday morning, as I lay in bed. *I have quite a lot of hair left. I was born in the First World. I am still not smoking.* I have been making this rapid survey of Things To Be Grateful For every morning since my heart attack. It's a variation on a ritual that I first devised when I was in Wormwood Scrubs. Prison wasn't as awful as I had pictured it. I got pushed about a couple of times in the dinner queue, but I was never actually beaten. And the two big-time mos in my wing both had a thing for black boys, thank you God. But I still used to wake every day in a breathless, claustrophobic panic, convinced that the walls of my cell were closing in on me, like one of those sado-masochistic almost-denouements in Batman. At first I used to cry and thrash about, but this made my cell-mate tetchy. So after a while I trained myself to lie very still and make mental lists of all the pleasant things that I would do when I got out. *Ring that woman I fucked in Wimbledon. Take the kids for a steak dinner.*

I watched a tiny tear of sweat making slow progress

down the side of Karen's neck. *Slightly creepy, that – the way the body keeps on doing its work while you rest: rumbling and oozing, the city that never sleeps. It would be more satisfactory if it shut down at night . . .*

Finally I got out of bed. Karen whimpered but remained asleep. This is one of the disadvantages of sharing your bed with young persons – they're so bloody good at the sleeping part. It makes you resentful. I have never objected to the much-scorned use of the phrase 'sleeping with' as a substitute for 'having sex with'. It only seems a coyness. The act of closing your eyes and slipping into unconsciousness with another person is infinitely more intimate and trusting a gesture – so much harder to pull off to both parties' satisfaction – than the jumping up and down on each other part. My wife was the only woman I have ever found entirely comfortable in this regard. She and I were a truly great sleeping partnership. We'd sleep with my prick nuzzling the cleavage of her bum, my hands cupping her big speckled breasts – or both of us in an overheated, face-to-face embrace, breathing in each other's fusty night breath. Once, we fell asleep while she was still down under the covers with my penis in her mouth, like a pacifier. That's how accomplished *we* were in the slumber department.

After I got up, I went to the master bathroom, where I mixed up a couple of spoonfuls of fibre powder ('for regularity and ease' the packet promises) with some bottled mineral water. Twirling the mixture with my toothbrush, I sidled up to and away from the full-length mirror next to the sink. Sissy Yerxa, my landlady, has a vooly for mirrors. The bathroom alone has three of them – this full-length, gilt-framed model and two others on opposing walls. The first night I arrived here, I took a bath and, as I was wrestling myself over the side, I saw my decrepit butt come rearing up at me in double reflection. Sheesh. What has been going on back there? Standing there in the bath, regarding my buttocks, I was reminded of the time, many years ago, when Oona found a bunch of rotting grapes at the back of the larder. 'Oh sweet!' she cried, holding out the little pulpless corpses. 'They're trying to become raisins!'

Since that bath-time revelation, I have grown obsessed with my withering body: my chest, for example, which, at some point when I wasn't paying attention, acquired breasts. Not perky little boobies mind you, but pendulous, Discovery Channel dugs. And my belly – oh, God, my belly! For a long time it was a sagging adjunct to the rest of me, which was fine. (At my age, only mos have flat stomachs.) But now it seems to be striving for absolute autonomy. Lately, when I lie on my back, I have noticed it swerving away, settling in a puddle of flesh at my side. In the mornings, I wake to find it lying next to me, gazing up at me, like an affectionate haggis.

I removed the toothbrush from the glass and drank back the fibre mixture. I paused for a moment, concentrating on not gagging, and then I stepped closer to the mirror, to examine my face. The whites of my eyes are yellow these days – as if someone has been pissing in them. My skin has the ancient, battered look of fried liver. My ears, which seem to have grown exponentially in recent months, are developing a violet tinge at their curly edges, like exotic salad leaves. I returned to the basin and hawked up three dime-sized gobs of khaki-coloured phlegm laced with black stuff, like – what is that stone? – like agate. A spider was lurking in the shadow of the plug. I reached for the tap, intending to wash it away, but the movement sent the spider careering madly around the slopes of the basin. I jumped back with a childish shriek. *Fuck that.*

I put on a robe, picked up my wash bag and walked along the veranda, to finish my ablutions in the guest suite. While I brushed my teeth, I gazed out of the little window above the sink. During the fortnight that I have been at

Casa De La Luna, I have been in the swimming pool only once, the day I arrived. My usual strategy in a pool is to lower myself in gradually, wade solemnly about for a few minutes and then get out. But on this occasion, as soon as I plopped in, Jesus, the houseboy, followed by Julia, the cook, rushed out to see the gringo having fun. With an audience willing me on, I felt obliged to perform. I did two lengths of slightly aggrandized doggy paddle before succumbing to a dramatic coughing fit. Then I climbed out and staggered about, panting '*Muy buen!*'

But they weren't fooled. I haven't been in since, and Karen doesn't go in either – the chlorine is bad for her hair or something. So now Jesus has decided that the pool is a legitimate corner to cut. The water has slowly turned milky, like an eye-cast. The Renaissance mosaic on the pool floor has become a Cubist blur, and around the edges of the pool there is a rotting border of bougainvillaea petals, dead insects and the egg-white gloop of frogspawn.

I must speak to Jesus about it. It's time I got things straight with that little bastard. For the money I'm paying, there are people who would have Jesus licking their boots clean. Already the servants have me pegged as a soft touch. When Sissy came over to welcome me to Puerto Vallarta – she stays in another place in the hills when she's renting out the villa – the servants couldn't run fast enough. Sissy has that skinny, gringo-bitch manner that these people respect.

So, okay. Some time this week I am going to take that little creep to one side.

'*Buenos Días, Jesus! The pool – it doesn't look so good. Perhaps you could . . .*'

No, no.

'*Ah! Jesus! Today, if you have time, could you . . .*'

Fuck that. Make it,

'*Jesus – come here and get this shit out of the pool.*'

*

The fibre drink was beginning to take effect. But I made myself hold out a little longer. These days I don't even attempt a crap until I've drunk some coffee to irritate my bowel into complete obeisance. The doctor who treated me for haemorrhoids last year gave me instructions about every aspect of the evacuation process. The cardinal rule is Never Strain. 'You want to wait until it's practically gliding out of your ass,' he told me. I have found that I rather enjoy observing his prescribed ritual. Sometimes, after a particularly satisfactory session, I stand watching the last, frantic pirouette of my turd before it disappears into the U-bend, and it's all I can do not to sing out in exaltation.

I have set up my computer in the living room on the ground floor of the villa. Here, for four or five hours every day, I sit hunched over a faux-Regency bureau with a cup of coffee, gazing at Sissy Yerxa's collection of the world's worst books. Theoretically I am hard at work, effecting the script changes requested by Hans Stempel. Mostly, though, what I do is pull disconsolately at my ears and review my sorry life. This morning, Reggie Boon rang up. Boon is under the impression that I am coping with the tragedy of my daughter's death by working like a fiend on his autobiography. Ever since the publishers told him about Sadie (to stop him agitating about the broken deadline) he has taken to calling me once or twice a week for soulful condolence-chats. Aside from boring the pants off me, his melancholy sighs and discreet allusions to the mystery of God's will make me feel horribly fraudulent. I tried my best today to keep him off the Sadie subject, but then he wanted to shoot the breeze about 'the creative process', which was really his delicate way of asking when the fuck I'm going to be done with his book. I humoured him for a little while – told him how stimulating I was finding it, translating the intricate subtleties of his personality into print. Then I pretended there was somebody at the door.

After he rang off, I tried to get down to some work. I fiddled with the brightness dial on my lap-top for a while. Then I tried to dislodge an old bagel crumb that was lurking between the O and P keys. Eventually I took out the paperback edition of my memoir, hoping to get some inspiration from the original material, or at least some reassurance from the thickness of the book. (See, Willy, you *can* write. Look at all those words you wrote by yourself.) The design is pure Seventies Tack: red matte cover with the title in portentously spaced, raised silver lettering.

To
Have
and
to
Hold

Hey, it could have been worse. Art, the idiot, wanted the American edition to be called *Fridge*.

Sadie and Sophie did not react well when the book was finally published. Sophie conscientiously tore her copy into a thousand pieces of jagged confetti, and sent them to me with a note that said, 'Stuff this up your bum'. Sadie wrote me a long letter explaining why I had Gone Too Far. Both girls declared their intention never to speak to me again. Sophie called me within the month, of course. To ask for money. But Sadie stuck to her guns. We never spoke again. She was like her mother in that respect – very disciplined about holding grudges. Years later, according to Monika, she continued to speak of the book as chief among my multiple sins – worse, even, than whatever had happened in the kitchen between her mother and me. This was pretty damn funny as far as I was concerned, given that the book paid for her and her sister's lousy educations and kept the two of them in lip gloss throughout their adolescences.

It's not as if I *wanted* to write the fucker. I had my share of torment about it. But I was broke. For my appeal, I had hired a new and fantastically expensive barrister – one of those old-Etonian socialists who only defend decadent pigs like me in order to subsidize their representation of immigrant yoghurt weavers, or whatever. I didn't like him much. I didn't like him at all, but he was a ruthless little bastard when it came to practising law, and that, believe me, is what you want when you're facing ten years of communal showers. Early on, he decided that the key to my case was establishing Oona as a drunk. The autopsy had pointed to a hair-raising blood alcohol level at the time of death, but the first guy had been afraid to make anything of this, for fear of looking like a shit. Jenks had no such scruples. He got together a bunch of witnesses to testify to Oona's being a lush, and then, as a kicker, he brought in a head-injury specialist to say that Oona's wounds were consistent with her having drunkenly smashed into the refrigerator all on her own. For these and other thoroughly unpleasant stratagems I paid him every penny I had. The night before I signed the publisher's contract, I remember lying in bed, rehearsing the endearingly candid explanations that I would murmur smoothly when challenged at dinner parties: '*Oh, you'd be surprised how an ethical dilemma loses its urgency when you've lost your job and the man at the dry-cleaner's starts refusing to cash your personal cheques . . .*' Even in the morning, as I drove to the publisher's with sheet marks impressed upon my sagging face,

I was uncertain as to whether I would really go through with it.

But I did. And in the end I found that, as with so many other disagreeable things in life, thinking about committing an ignominious, vulgar action is a great deal worse than the actual execution of said action. Publication was uncomfortable – no doubt about it. You wouldn't think it to see me now, but I used to be quite a popular figure in the London media crowd. Oona and I – with our fucked-up Volvo and our Columbian pottery and our orange cookware – we were just the sort of couple that people wanted over at their house on a Friday evening eating their *osso buco* and drinking their rather interesting red wines. The book put an end to all that. There were a couple of people in the beginning who made a great thing of 'rallying round', but when the serial rights were purchased by one of the tabloids – the same one, in fact, that dubbed me 'Wicked Willy' during the police hunt – even the rally-rounders drifted away. (It was one thing to be loyal to a man suspected of killing his wife – potentially rather cool, in fact – quite another to be associated with a man selling tales of his 'Marriage from Hell' to the gutter press.) As I say, though, it wasn't so bad. I found a certain liberty in my disgrace. It was as if, having been tested once, and found so sorely wanting, I was now forever exempt from any cramping expectation of good taste or virtue. *If I am a shit*, I used to tell myself defiantly in those days – *so be it*.

I ended up re-reading quite a bit of the book this morning.

The house was in darkness when I arrived home that Monday night. This was not unusual. One of the ways in which Oona's depression manifested itself was with her intolerance of light, as if seeking from the exterior world a reflection of the gloom she felt within. I hung my coat up and walked down the corridor towards the living room, feeling the familiar sense of foreboding. There was a prickly, almost electric, feeling in the air that, in our household, always presaged an argument.

In the living room, I found Oona crouched on the sofa, unbathed and wearing a soiled and unironed dress. She had been drinking. This was also no surprise. Cocktail hour came very early in our house, back then. Despite my repeated efforts to get her to seek help, Oona's depression had been growing deeper throughout that winter.

As I entered, she looked up and began to whimper. She had been crying. Her make-up was streaked.
'Darling . . .' I began, but I could not finish. What was there to say? I still longed to rescue my wife from the tunnel of despair into which she was fast disappearing, but at long last I had come to recognize the truth of what Dr Collar had told me: if Oona was to be saved, it really was only she who could save herself.

'Where are the girls?' I asked.

'With Monika,' she replied, referring to their aunt. Often, when Oona felt too miserable to function, she would call my sister and ask her to pick the children up from school. I went over to the phone to call Monika and see that the girls were all right. As I did so, Oona got up and began weaving uncertainly towards the drinks cabinet. I could hear the afternoon's intake sloshing about inside her. 'Darling, please,' I said. 'Not another one.'

She did not reply. She did not turn around. She laughed. It was a cold, angry laugh – a laugh that seemed to sum up just how radically and irreversibly things had changed since that rainy day, fifteen years previously, when I had met her, a sweet, sad girl in a pink

*mackintosh that was too big for her, sheltering under
a tree in Hyde Park. I knew now, as certainly as I have
ever known anything, that our marriage was beyond
repair.*

*I sank slowly into an armchair and sat for a few
moments, listening to her drunkenly banging about in the
kitchen. Then I called Monika. Everything was fine. The
girls were watching cartoons. Would it be better, she
asked, if they stayed the night over there?*

'Well . . . would that be okay with you?' I asked.

She sighed. 'Yes, fine.'

*From the direction of the drinks cabinet there came a
loud crash. I said goodbye and got up, concerned that
Oona might have hurt herself.*

'Are you okay in there?' I called.

*She responded with a volley of expletives. This was
what our marriage had come to . . .*

As always when reading my own work, I was slightly taken
aback by the authority of my own bad prose. How credibly
I write schlock! How seamlessly I have translated real life
– *my* real life – into this airport drivel! I turned now to
Chapter Six, entitled, 'The Last Argument'.

*. . . In the kitchen, she was sitting on the floor against
the cooker. She glared up at me, hatred imprinted on her
face. I bent down to help her, but she pushed me away
angrily, almost causing me to topple over. I was too
worried and sick at heart to want an argument, so I
stood up and began to leave the kitchen again.*

*As I reached the door, I felt a sharp blow to the back
of my neck. Oona had stood up now and was attacking
me. 'You bastard,' she hissed, her arms flailing. I covered
my face with my arms to protect myself from the
onslaught, but she managed to jab one of her fingers into*

my eye. Then she slipped. Some patch of grease on the kitchen linoleum made her lose her footing and she careened away from me. It is a cliché to describe these things as occurring in slow motion. But clichés are clichés because they are true. I watched, horrified, as Oona smashed her head against the handle of the refrigerator door and then sank to the floor. The kitchen was very silent all of a sudden. I could hear a small boy, outside, in the garden next door, shouting gaily and, further away, in the next street, a dog barking. Oona's eyes were closed. Blood was seeping slowly from the wound at the back of her skull. Even before I bent down to feel her pulse, I knew she was going to die.

In private moments of vanity, I sometimes try to persuade myself that it costs me effort to write this badly. But that's not quite right. I know, even as I am writing, that it is awful stuff. That's something, I suppose. But it's not as if there are faucets of inspiration that I have to turn off, or *mots justes* that I have sighingly to throw away. The crap just bubbles out of me, uncorrupted. Bad writing is my gift.

I leafed through some more papers now and got out a copy of the letter that Hans Stempel had sent to the studio about my screenplay. At the top of the page, Phil Buscemi had clipped a covering note.

Dear Willy,
Here are Stempel's thoughts on your first draft. I thought you'd appreciate hearing them 'from the horse's mouth'. As you can see, he is as excited as we are. Let me know what you think.
Phil

I unclipped the note and read the letter.

Dear Phillip,
It was great to speak with you yesterday. As you
requested I have jotted down some of my initial thoughts
on *To Have and to Hold*. I really think this can be a
great movie. It has a fabulous arc and it holds out the
promise that finally we can see an adult picture about the
complicatedness and contradictions of married life! Let's
try to make it happen!

1. One immediate concern is that the screenplay has too
much in the domestic vein at the moment. As it now
stands, the first act is entirely devoted to home matters. I
think we should establish the situation – that the wife is
an alcoholic and a bitch and that he has been putting up
with a lot of shit – much quicker and then move straight
into the refrigerator sequence and the whole 'on the run'
segment.

2. The references to his affairs are too oblique at the
moment. It would be nice if we could actually see him in
bed with a girlfriend – laughing, making love, drinking
champagne – so that we introduce something a little bit
sexy and also, we get a chance to see the potentiality that
is being repressed in the marriage.

3. Is there any way we can replace the refrigerator with
some more cinematic death?

4. The courtroom scenes don't hold my attention. Too
much legal stuff, not enough drama. Also, we are missing
an opportunity with the prison sequences. They should
be more brutal, more degraded. Perhaps someone tries to
fuck him up the ass?

5. After his release, much more is needed about the hypocrisy of the London society – maybe a scene where he goes to a party and everybody snubs him. We should get a strong sense that yesterday, he was 'king of the hill' and now, he is an 'untouchable'.

6. Possibly my strongest concern at the moment, is that the protagonist is not vivid enough. This is very important. We need Willy to incarnate all the masculine vigour that English society wants to destroy. Perhaps, there should be a monologue from him in which he makes explicit his conflicts, his anguish in his marriage. This is a movie that can potentially strike a chord with a lot of guys out there! He is an existentialist hero – let us make him a little more defiant!

7. Finally, there has to be another woman in his life. I like the idea of him coming to America at the end, but not alone! I think there should be a lady to share this wonderful new life with him! I see a young, innocent woman with an old soul – someone who has the strength of mind to ignore society and love him in spite of everything.

There is much more to say of course, but these are the really major issues that strike me right now. I look forward to your feedback.

Yours,
Hans Stempel

After I had finished reading the letter, I laid my head down on the desk.

To be despised and forsaken for one's despicable acts is not so bad, really. It is being forgiven, understood – *identified with*, for Christ's sake – by someone like this Hans Stempel that is truly insufferable. When the book was first published, I got a lot of nasty reviews saying I was a lowlife trying to make money out of my wife's death. But the only time I ever got really upset was when I received a favourable review in the *Evening Standard*. The man called it a 'searing, painfully honest account of one man's journey into disaster', 'a compelling look at the dark underbelly of modern marriage' and 'a classy kiss-and-tell'. Stempel's letter reminds me of that review. There is no act you can commit in this world so heinous that it won't attract its own little cult of losers and loons. Stempel is just a slightly more privileged version of those 300lb crazy-women who send love letters to paedophiles on Death Row.

7

4 June 1974

*Dad sent Sophie a hundred dollars from America. She
showed me the card. It had a picture of a little monkey
with a sad face on the front and inside it said Have you
forgiven me? Love Dad. She said she didn't ask for it. I just
said oh yeah, do reckon. I think Dad must have practised
with his handwriting. He normally has crappy, scratchy
handwriting, but for this, it was all billowy, poetic,
father-penning-a-missive-to-his-daughter-y. What a
wanker. Sophie was talking to Aunt Monika the other day
and Monika said his life would be intolerable if he lived
here so we shouldn't blame him. They're nicer to people
like Dad over there, she said. Sophie is on the dole at the
moment and living with Mick at his mum's house in
Kennington. Last week it was half term and I really didn't
want to go to Leeds so she let me go with her and her
friends to a music festival in Wiltshire. We stayed in a field
for two nights. I didn't have a very nice time. Everyone
took a lot of drugs, including Sophie even though she is
pregnant. I didn't because Sophie said I was too young.
They all behaved really silly. Also, Sophie kept running
away to snog Mick. The tent was horrid and cold and you
couldn't have a shower and when you wanted to go to the
loo, you had to queue for hours to go in a Portakabin with
pooh everywhere. A lot of people went outside but I just
held it in. When I got back to Aunt Monika's, my bath was
black. On the second night this old American hippy called
Albert wearing a sarong started talking to me. He was very*

sweet. He gave me his cushion to sit on while we were watching the bands and afterwards he took me to his tent which he had all to himself. He smoked some grass and I had some too!!! I didn't really like the taste but I smoked quite a bit. He started telling me how beautiful I was. I don't think he knew how young I was. He asked if I wanted to do acid but I said no and he said cool. He had long hair (grey) in a bun. He must have been nearly fifty and his teeth were yukky. He said that he hadn't been to a dentist since he was sixteen years old. He was nice to me though. When he kissed me, I was a bit horrified because of his horrible flappy lip and his yellow teeth and the grey bun but I closed my eyes and I felt quite sexy. Then he undid his trousers and took out his willy. Look isnt it beautiful he said. I nearly died!! He took off my sweatshirt and just stared at me. I was so embarassed. Then he tried to have sex with me but I said no and he said cool again. Then he put his willy away and we smoked some more grass and he asked would I just pleasure him? He meant wank him off. I was really scared because I didn't know how to do it, but he showed me and it was OK. His yukky sperm went all over my sweatshirt. It smelled of chemicals. Later when I went back to our tent, Sophie said in front of everyone, Eurghh, you didn't fuck that hippie did you? She can be so bitchy sometimes.

I sat in the living room until midday. Then I came out and had lunch with Karen on the veranda. We ate salad and tacos prepared by Julia and drank bottled beer. Karen, who had spent the morning lying by the pool, brought to the lunch table a pungent odour of coconut tanning oil. Her freckles, I noticed, have grown more profuse than ever. She looks like a very pale person peering through a ginger scrim.

'Do you want to go for a drive somewhere this afternoon?' she asked.

Sure, I want to ride round the hot streets of Smellyville,
Mexico, talking to you.

'No,' I said.

After lunch, she trooped back to her sun-lounger and I
went to my bedroom for a short nap. I have been wondering,
lately, whether perhaps I ought to see a shrink. Just before I
left California, Penny referred quite casually to my 'mid-life
crisis' as if it were an acknowledged certainty that that is
what I am going through. I got very angry with her and
pointed out that unless I am destined to live to 110 (please
God, no) the statute of limitations on mid-life crises ran
out for me some time ago. She just stroked my head and
said that I was a very special person and oughtn't to be so
hard on myself. All that aside, I am going to have to do
something, sooner or later, about this slump I am in.

I have been to two shrinks in my life. The first, in Culver
City, was Dr Krakower, an orthodox Freudian with an
office that smelt of cherry air-freshener and a habit of
repeatedly forgetting seminal points of my biography.
Initially, I resisted the offensive suggestion that my narra-
tives were too boring for her to retain, but when, after
sixteen weeks and thirty-two sessions, I found myself having
to remind her of my late wife's name, I decided to call it
quits. My second and last shrink was a guy out in the
Valley, recommended by Art. Rudy Bupnick was his name
– he liked me to call him Rudy. He did not subscribe to
any one school of psychiatry. ('I prefer,' he said during
the first session, 'to take a little from everywhere, like a
honey-bee.') I don't know if he was a fully paid-up mo, but
he was certainly of mo-like demeanour. He wore orange
pants made of some textured velveteen material. His whole
office was done out in contrasting shades of pink. He talked
a great deal, which seemed, at first, to be a good thing –
an improvement, certainly, on the dank silences of Dr
Krakower's office. But the novelty began to fade after a

month or so, when I realized that I had not the slightest clue what Bupnick was talking *about*. He had this very metaphorical way of talking, combined with a hushed, almost conspiratorial delivery. 'As you *know*,' he was always murmuring, in a way that made you loath to admit that you really did *not* know. He had this one conceit in particular, about the need for me to close a door – a trapdoor – which he always accompanied with a strenuous opening and shutting gesture of his hands. 'As you *know*, what is really important for you right now is that you take that attic trapdoor and *slam* it shut. Once and for all.' By the time I realized quite how central a role this trope was going to play in my therapy, Bupnick had used it a million times and I was simply too embarrassed to ask what it meant.

The only thing I have retained from my expensive hours in Bupnick's office is his manifestly fallacious theory on my relationship with Oona. Bupnick believed that in every marriage there is a master and a slave. The roles may be exchanged from time to time, but at any given moment there is always one supplicant spouse and one who is calling the shots. On the basis of what he knew about my philandering, Bupnick concluded that I had been the bossy boots in my marriage, and Oona the put-upon pussy-cat. I didn't like to say so at the time, but he had it all wrong. Oona and I would have liked to have played things that way, but we were never able to pull it off. Oona wanted to be told what to do, but she couldn't, in actual fact, bear a single instruction. Her termagant nature simply rebelled. I wanted to be a task-master – a stern, bacon-bringing, craggy-faced man of the house. But the slightest hint of resistance from my not-so-little woman and I was ready to chuck in the whole Charlton Heston act for a quiet life. There was also the unhappy but incontrovertible fact that Oona was better at arguing than me. I don't mean that she was quicker-witted. Or more skilled in devising jaw-dropping insults. (Heaven forfend.) She simply had a superior commitment to the fight. Oona gave herself to an argument with more determination and passion than any woman (or man) I've ever known. The kind of prevaricating, amateurish delicacy that advises against saying things in anger that you might later regret was not for Oona. In the roar and crash of battle, she would say literally anything: that your breath revolted her, that your appearances on television were 'embarrassing', that she fancied one of your colleagues. The point of an argument, as she saw it, was to inflict pain. And if a job was worth doing, it was worth doing with unimaginable spleen. You could try to top her – with vicious reports on the deterioration of her figure, or the revolting way she chewed her food. But she wasn't to be out-nastied. Never, in the fifteen years I lived with her, was there a single moment when I got her to step back with the gratifyingly flummoxed, watery expression of someone truly hurt.

Once, when we were on honeymoon and all this anguish was before us, we overheard an elderly Jewish couple bickering in one of the corridors of the Algonquin. This old codger, with his nylon slacks pulled up to his tits, was giving his wife a hard time for leading him the wrong way to the elevator. 'Everything you know!' he kept muttering sarcastically. 'Everything you know! I told you it was the other way already, but you wouldn't listen to me. Oh no, everything you know!' The woman tramped along absorbing his wrath, and then, in a little voice, she squawked back defiantly, 'Everything *you* know!'

Oona, who was new enough to marriage to find marital squabbling cute, kept referring to this exchange all that week. 'Everything you know!' she would shout at me, dancing around me as we walked down the street. 'Everything you know! Everything you know!'

*

When I woke from my nap, there was someone knocking at my door. I ignored it. Karen has a habit of coming to my room during my afternoon nap to proffer sex. I couldn't face turning her down again. Since my heart attack, I have made several incomplete attempts at intercourse with both Penny and Karen. I've wanted to do it – or rather, I've wanted to want to. But on each occasion I have found myself too weary and *distrait* to go through with the thing. The doctor at the Beverly Memorial told me, in a rather excruciating *hombre a hombre* before I checked out, that some recovering cardiac patients unconsciously resist achieving orgasm for fear of inducing another attack. This, he said, was a quite understandable but entirely unfounded fear: if anything, he would recommend ejaculation as a useful way of regulating stress. All very well and good – but irrelevant in my case. My penis isn't *scared*. It's bored. It lounges about like a jaded Arab princeling, and nothing – not the prize features of Art's porn collection, nor the combined efforts of Penny and Karen – can rouse it from its inscrutable lassitude. Both women have insisted that they don't care, that it is no big deal. Which means, of course, that they care a lot. Karen, I sense, is particularly distraught about the coital failures – her disappointment being less a matter of her own sexual frustration than an agitation about failing in the one service she has been brought along to provide. 'Let's have another go,' she keeps demanding, in a singularly wilting fashion. 'It'll get better, I promise.'

I very much doubt that it will. I am sceptical about the efficacy of 'practice' when it came to sexual matters. In my experience, first times are peaks and everything thereafter is a slow but inexorable descent towards boredom and repulsion. I would go so far as to suggest that the law of diminishing returns dictates the trajectory of sexual experience in general. This is counter to the received wisdom, I know. But personally, I do not expect to ever match, let alone surpass, the exquisite results of rubbing myself up and down, aged twelve, on a knubbly yellow blanket in my mother's bedroom.

There was another knock at the door now. I remained silent and very still. Then I heard the door open. *For crying out loud, take a hint why don't you?* I was lying on my side, with my back to the doorway, but I shut my eyes anyway. It occurred to me that it might be Jesus standing there. Perhaps the little bastard was contemplating the theft of my watch which was lying on the bedside table. I heard my name being whispered: Karen, after all. I tensed my body into absolute quietness. A couple of seconds passed. It's amazing what concentration pretending to be asleep requires. Then, quite suddenly, I lost my temper. 'For Christ's sake, Karen,' I said, without turning over. 'I'm trying to sleep here.'

I waited for her sniffled reproach, but there was none – only the shuffle of feet and the sound of the door being closed very carefully, like someone replacing the lid on a jewellery box. I was instantly sorry. Being mean to Karen is a lot more trouble in the long run than counting to ten and being nice. Now I would have to affect feelings of shame and penitence. Give her a big cheque to go and buy more useless trash from the Pinyata Club. Humour her wittering for the entire evening. I heard her go downstairs – sounding rather heavy for Karen, who usually has a fluttering, barefoot tread. Then I heard voices floating up through the floorboards, from the dining room below.

'Is there anything to drink?' a male voice asked. I rolled over and looked at my watch. Richard and Heidi were supposed to arrive at the airport at six. It was only four – they must have got in early. I sat up, preparing to go down and play host – then I lay back down again. Fuck it – I

68

could leave them with Karen for another ten minutes or so. Richard would probably appreciate having a babe breathe on him for a bit.

'How is he?' I heard him ask now.

'He was asleep.' It was a female voice, but it didn't sound like Karen or Heidi. 'I didn't think I should wake him.' No, definitely not Karen. I began to feel a prickling at the base of my spine.

Oh shit. Oh *shit*.

It was Penny.

I strained to hear what was being said.

'So you didn't get to talk to him?' another female voice – Karen's – asked.

'No.' (Penny's voice, sounding pissed off.) 'Like I said, I didn't think I should wake him.' *Good girl*. For a moment, I had thought she was going to make trouble by repeating what I had said. There was another long pause. The girls were definitely not hitting it off down there. 'So did you come out here with him?' That was Penny.

'Uh-huh.' That was Karen.

'Well, how *nice*.' Penny again. Oh shitshitshit.

I sat up and considered what to do. Penny has caught me cheating on her once or twice in the past. But, until now, all her discoveries have been made by way of credit-card statements or phone numbers scrawled in match-books. She has never nabbed me in the act before.

Just as I was reconciling myself to the necessity of going downstairs, there was another knock at the door and Richard came in.

'Hey fat boy,' he said. 'We got an earlier plane . . .'

I dislike being called names. Richard knows this. I nearly hit him once, when he called me – I hesitate to repeat the foul epithet – 'needle dick'. But, still, he persists.

'Has what I think happened, happened?' I interrupted.

Richard nodded and began to laugh. I watched stone-faced as he snorted and shook. I really do not like Richard much.

'Close the door, will you?' I asked at last.

'Hey, I'm sorry,' Richard said, shutting the door and coming to sit on my bed. 'She got back from her shoot early and she wanted to come. We thought it would be a nice surprise for you. I had no idea you'd brought Miss Freckle along . . .' He began laughing again. 'You should see it downstairs. It's scary.'

'Have you got a cigarette?' I asked. I didn't like the dismissive way he called Karen 'Miss Freckle'. Like he didn't even rate her. The envious little fuck.

He got out a pack from his breast pocket and passed me one. 'When did you start smoking again?' he asked, flicking a lighter.

'Now,' I said miserably.

I must say, I rather like the way I smoke. Unlike most heavy smokers, I communicate immense enjoyment when I am consuming my drug. I hold the cigarette in the squaddie style, between thumb and forefinger, and suck deeply, lustily. I usually allow the smoke to stay in my lungs for a while – several seconds at least – before dropping my jaw and exhaling. Then, as the smoke finally escapes from my mouth in a thin, lilac-grey swirl, I re-inhale it one more delicious time through my nose. People often stop what they're doing to gaze, as Richard did now, at the spectacle of my pleasure.

'How are you going to deal with this?' he asked.

'Fuck knows,' I said. 'How does Penny look like she's taking it?'

'Well, not great. But she's pretty contained, right now.'

I took a last pull on the cigarette and dropped it in the glass of water at my bedside. (I have truly revolting smoking manners.) 'Okay,' I said to Richard, 'we better go down.'

When we arrived in the living room, Heidi and Penny

were standing in a corner, admiring one of Sissy Yerxa's execrable pieces of Mexican folk art. Heidi, who fancies herself something of an art connoisseur, was busy talking nonsense. Penny was standing next to her, with her head cocked and a hooked forefinger pressed against her lips – her cultured-person stance.

Karen was perched on the sofa at the other end of the room, looking nervous. 'Hi,' I said in as jovial a manner as I could muster. All three of them turned and looked at Richard and me for a silent moment. 'Well,' Heidi murmured, loud enough for everyone to hear. 'The Lothario awakes.' Penny rushed forward with arms outstretched.

'Baby!'

The next second she was clamped against me, her stiff hair grating my cheek, the taste of her face-powder in my mouth. 'Oh, *Willy*,' she whispered in my ear. 'You *have* been naughty.' I was confused. I knew Penny was not the type to make a public scene – but I'd been expecting at least a little flounciness. This cheery, conspiratorial manner came from out of left field. Over her shoulder, I could see Karen, all freckly bafflement, and Heidi, her eyebrows flexed in sardonic amusement, both staring at our clinch.

I pulled away and went over to Heidi to kiss her. She was wearing black and white jogging pants and a preposterous pair of silver tennis shoes. (Apparently, one of the requirements of working in the youth-music industry is that you dress like a clown.) 'So!' I said, 'I see everyone's met. How was the flight? Are you exhausted? What about a drink? Who wants a margarita?'

Everybody, it seemed, wanted a margarita, but first, Penny needed to freshen up a little. She insisted on using the upstairs bathroom. (To snoop about, no doubt, and confirm that Karen was sleeping in my bedroom.) Karen, Richard and Heidi were left in the living room while I hustled into the kitchen to start mixing the drinks. The sleeping arrangements were clearly going to be the big issue here. What to do? There is another guest room upstairs, next to my bedroom, but Penny could hardly be expected to sleep there and I couldn't just boot Karen out of my bed, could I? I hadn't been in the kitchen a minute before Karen appeared. 'What's going on, Willy?' she asked, zooming towards me, with alarming intensity and speed. 'You didn't tell me that Penny woman was coming.'

'No,' I said, with forced casualness, leaning into the refrigerator for some limes. 'I didn't know she was. This is a surprise.'

'Is she . . .' Karen paused. 'Are you guys in a relationship?'

God, how I hate it when women get feisty and direct about stuff.

'What do you mean?' I said, stalling, my head still in the refrigerator.

'What do you mean what do I mean?' Karen said. 'You know what I mean. Are you guys in a relationship? Are you sleeping with each other?'

'Oh for God's sake, Karen!' I roared suddenly. Then, remembering Richard and Heidi out in the living room, I shifted into a hissed whisper. 'Could we talk about this later?'

Of course we couldn't. 'What?' she yapped. 'What did I say? What are *you* so pissed off about?'

I experienced a strong desire to smack her across the face. But of course I didn't. I didn't do anything. I kept quiet.

'Oh, I'm *sorry*,' she went on. 'Why should it be any of my business, if some stupid bitch comes walking in here and starts practically frenching you? God, how, like, totally *unreasonable* of me, to ask who she is!'

She stopped – her limited store of sarcastic retort now exhausted – and stood at the kitchen counter regarding me furiously while I feigned intense involvement in the business of making the drinks.

'Willy! she shouted at last, 'are you going to tell me what's going on, or not?'

'Look! Keep it down, will you?' I pleaded, knowing, even as I did so, that this would only encourage her to raise the volume further. There was a long silence. And then, at a pitch that must surely have carried out into the living room, beyond that to the downstairs lavatory and way down to the little shed at the end of the garden where the servants sit when they have nothing to do, Karen screamed, 'Well, fuck you, Willy – you little piece of shit!'

With that, she rushed away. I stayed in the kitchen, finishing off the drinks, and then I shuffled out into the living room with a pitcher of margarita and a tray of glasses.

'She's down at the pool,' Heidi said dryly, as I looked around for Karen.

'Ah,' I said. Then I smiled in what I hoped was an appealingly rueful way: 'I'm sorry about all this.' Richard made 'No need to apologize' noises. Heidi just looked at me. She didn't think I was appealing, I could tell. As I set down the pitcher and tray, I could smell the sourness of my own perspiration.

Penny descended from the bathroom now. 'What was *that*?' she asked, all innocent concern. 'Was that your friend shouting? Is she okay?'

'Yes, everything's fine,' I muttered. 'Here, have a drink.'

We all sat down then, and talked for a while. Enquiries were made about my health. Some scurrilous gossip about various TV personalities was provided by Richard. Penny told a number of dreary and altogether pointless anecdotes about the commercial shoot she had just finished working on. (Out of relief and gratitude to her for behaving so well, I laughed exorbitantly at all of them.) Presently, Julia arrived to start preparations for dinner, and Richard and

Heidi took this as their cue to repair for showering and unpacking. I took them out to the guest house by the pool. (Karen was lying on a lounger with her eyes shut. She did not stir as we passed.) Then I came back into the villa, expecting to have it out with Penny.

I found her kneeling on the living-room floor, unzipping one of her fake Louis Vuitton suitcases.

'What are you doing?' I asked.

She looked up, smiling. 'Me?'

'Yes, you.' This showy insouciance of hers was beginning to freak me.

'Oh, I'm just picking out something to wear for dinner,' she said.

I stood there watching her as she picked through her neatly folded clothes. Less than an hour ago, she had arrived in Mexico to find me shacking up with some pink-haired floozie twenty years her junior, and now she was having to sort out her evening-wear choices on the floor of the living room. Was she really not going to say anything? After a while she looked up.

'Don't stand there staring at me like that!' she protested in a friendly, almost playful way. 'I'll get self-conscious!'

Karen now appeared at the French windows. She gazed for a moment at Penny and me, then she swished past us and up the stairs. Presently, we heard the door to the master suite being slammed. Penny grimaced. 'Gee,' she said, 'she has an awful lot of freckles, doesn't she?'

Dinner that night was tense. Penny, who had made a unilateral decision to install herself in the guest bedroom, spent nearly an hour locked away performing her toilette before descending in a spangled black cocktail dress, gold sandals and a lot of pink lipstick. Karen, on the other hand, came to the table ostentatiously drab in pig-tails and sweat pants – the Hollywood princess's approximation of a hair-shirt. We got through most of the meal okay. Karen and

Penny didn't eat. (Karen was too busy being upset and Penny doesn't do meals, preferring to nibble and suck on a long, skinny line of non-fat, low-cal snacks throughout the day.) Heidi talked at length about a recent sex scandal involving a pop singer with whom everyone apart from me seemed to be familiar. Richard told a dirty story about a famous Hollywood actress. Both he and Heidi tried a couple of times to draw Karen into the conversation, but she just sat there, pale and unhappy as veal, refusing to do anything other than murmur yes and no. Then, during dessert, Penny started talking about a holiday that she and I took together a couple of years ago in St Bart's. Apparently, some woman we met there had told us she had a house in Puerto Vallarta. Penny wanted to know if she could look her up. I was trying to remember who this woman was, when I noticed that Karen had begun to cry. Fat tears were plopping silently on to her untouched plate of mango. Everyone else noticed too, I guess, but no one said anything. Penny continued banging on about this old bag from St Bart's and then Heidi described some new hotel on the island that she'd read about in a magazine. Soon, Karen began to shake with silent sobs. This was too much for me. (Like most men, I tend to harden, rather than soften, at the sight of female tears.) I stood up abruptly.

'Hey, I'm sorry,' I said to the assembled company. 'The invalid seems to be getting a little sleepy. I think I'm going to turn in now.'

'Yeah – you get some rest, sweetie,' Penny said, proprietorially.

Karen continued to look down at her plate and blub.

'Richard,' Heidi said heavily, 'we should be thinking about turning in too, don't you think?' That's Heidi – queen of the interrogative command. Richard didn't want to leave – he suspected there was going to be a cat fight and he wanted to be there to see it. But Heidi's tone brooked no debate. Reluctantly, he scraped his chair back from the table and got up. 'Yeah,' he said. 'I guess it *has* been a long day.'

'Well, goodnight all,' I said in the stupid, hearty tone that I had been keeping up all afternoon.

'Oh, Willy,' Richard said, as I started up the stairs. 'Could I come up and borrow some of that insect repellent you were telling me about?' This was his ruse to come upstairs and gossip. Christ, what a *girl*. I nodded without turning round, and when I reached the first floor I stopped and waited for him. He wasn't far behind. When he reached my side, he immediately began punching the air and jogging up and down. 'Oh, man,' he exclaimed in a gleeful whisper. 'Oh, *man*.'

I shut my eyes and shook my head in an obliging show of mock-despair. (Sometimes, it's easier just to submit.)

'Willy, what the hell are you going to do?' Richard asked. His face was lit up like a Christmas tree.

'I don't know,' I muttered.

'The *shit* you get yourself into . . .'

'I know. I know,' I said. 'Listen, has Penny said anything to you and Heidi?'

He shook his head. 'Nope.'

'Well, what do you think she's playing at? She hasn't said a word to me about Karen and she's been sweet all afternoon.'

'Ach, Penny's smart,' Richard said. 'She's got it worked out . . .' An idea now occurred to him. 'Hey! Play it right, Willy,' he leered, 'and maybe you can get the two of them in your bed tonight.'

'Yeah,' I said. 'Maybe.'

I was suddenly sick of him. 'Look, I've got to get some sleep. I'll see you in the morning.'

Before he could reply, I walked into my bedroom and closed the door.

For a long time, I lay on my bed, trying to summon up the energy to brush my teeth. I was surprised by how genuinely dejected I felt. There was a time when a sexual farce such as this would have gratified me intensely – more, perhaps, than the sex itself. Now I would have paid handsomely to have the whole tawdry business taken off my hands. I kept picturing Richard out in the guest house, already planning how to manufacture the episode into future dinner-table anecdote. From downstairs, there came a low buzz of female talk. If I listened carefully, I could make out some of what was being said.

'I feel so bad,' I heard Karen saying. 'I had no idea . . . I'm so sorry.' She was still weeping.

Then Penny said, 'You know something? It's okay. Really. Don't be so upset. You haven't done anything wrong.'

Christ, amazing – Penny intellectually dominating a situation. There was some more talk now, but it was too muted for me to make out. I felt excited and, at the same time, oddly emasculated, lying there, straining to hear what they were saying about me. Then I distinctly heard Penny say, 'Lookit, you mustn't fret – Willy *told* me he was bringing you.'

'He did?'

I pictured Karen's jaw falling.

'Sure. Me and Willy, we . . . we have an understanding.'

Richard was right. Oh, clever Penny.

I wondered who would end up coming to join me in bed. I wondered whom I would *prefer* to come to bed. The two women have very different styles. Penny regards male sexuality as a pitifully simple mechanism – the libidinal equivalent of wind-up chattering teeth. She has an unshakeable faith in the power of knickers and stockings and knock-out clouds of 'fragrance'. She possesses a vast wardrobe of seduction garments – shortie nylon nighties comprised of multiple translucent layers, slithery satin teddies that pop apart at the crotch, ribboned, 'wench'-style corsets beaded with fake pearls. She wears full make-up to bed. (In the morning, the pillows are always daubed beige and black.) She maintains a terrifying set of pearl-pink talons for sexual back-scrawling. Karen, on the other hand, is a modern girl. Her underwear is white, seamless cotton, and she takes it off briskly before she comes to bed. She smells of soap and some sort of lemon-perfumed skin cream. Her face is scrubbed pink and her pubic hair is always shaved to an oblong strip of strawberry-blonde stubble – like fuzzy felt.

Downstairs, I could hear that Karen was sobbing again. Penny was cooing comfort. 'Are you in love with him?' she asked. I couldn't hear Karen's reply, but it must have been affirmative, because next Penny said, in a wonderful tone of deep-throated regret, 'Oh sweetheart. You poor thing. I didn't realize. I'm so sorry.'

The mysterious maundering of the voices went on and on – for hours, it seemed. Just before I succumbed to sleep, it occurred to me, with a little tingle of disappointment and relief, that neither woman was going to be coming into my bed that night.

When I awoke this morning, Karen was walking around my bedroom, packing her things. She was wearing one of my shirts, throwing her clothes into a case with angry little flourishes.

She's learned how to do this from watching movies, I thought.

'You're going?' I said.

She began to cry. I lay watching her in silence. *Christ, how much salt water does this woman have in her?*

'I'm very sorry about all this,' I said, finally.

She dropped the dress she was folding and rushed at me.

I thought she was going to attack me – but she only fell softly on the bed and pressed her wet, hot face against mine. I could feel her tears trickling down my chest. One found its way to my belly button. Suddenly, I was drastically in need of sex. I lay for a moment, with my eyes closed, feeling my penis unfurl, wondering if it was too impossibly evil to do what I was about to do. She was pressing closer to me – laying her leg across me.

'Get on top of me,' I muttered, at last. My eyes were still closed. I felt her hesitate – felt her gazing up at me pinkly. Then I opened my eyes and she was unbuttoning her shirt.

8

11 May 1976

*Sophie broke up with Mick and she has taken Jack to
live in a squat in the Elephant & Castle. She already has
a new boyfriend so she is not that upset. Miss Gordon
wrote to Aunt Margaret saying that I have become
difficult and anti-social and that I told her I didn't want
to stay on at Hazlitt's after 'O' levels next year. What a
silly cow. Aunt Margaret had a shit-fit and said I had to
start seeing a therapist again. She wrote to Dad and told
him he had to pay for it if he didn't want me turning out
like Sophie. So now I get to go into town every week
instead of doing games. Ha ha. My new therapist is
called Doctor Robinson. He is not all that bad. He's got
a voice that makes you feel slightly tired and relaxed.
Also, he sometimes says quite funny things. But it's all
pointless. Therapists never seem to have anything bad to
say about you, only about the other people. They always
believe the wrong things. When I was little, I used to
make up stories for Doctor Brock about how I saw mum
dead on the floor, with bits of her head all around her.
I'm not sure why I did that. I think I just wanted to be
entertaining. And then when I would tell him I was only
messing about, he would go very serious and act as if I
was about a step away from jumping out of a window.
Dr Robinson likes me to talk about Dad but I am really
sick of the subject. Sophie is always going on about it —
she says he has abandoned us — but she is so fake. We are
the ones who told him to fuck off.*

Dr Robinson says I'm blocking. He is so stupid, it gets on my nerves.

'Was your father an alcoholic?' he asked today.

'Well, no,' I said, 'not . . .'

'No?'

'No. I don't know what he's like now but when I knew him he wasn't an alcoholic. He always drank a lot. But he ate a lot. He smoked a lot.'

'You have told me that he sometimes drank several glasses of Grand Marnier before midday.'

'Yes, that's true, but . . .'

'Yes?'

'. . . when you say alcoholic like that, it seems like . . . you know, all these labels. I mean, he wasn't drunk all the time or anything . . .'

'Sadie.'

'He didn't roll around, smashing things up. He worked every day.'

'Why do you resist the idea that your father was an alcoholic? Do you want to protect him?'

I just know it will irritate me later on if I don't describe it properly. But he gets annoyed, as if I'm being stubborn. Brock was like that too. When I try to tell the truth, I am told I am not doing it right. In the end I give him what he wants. Its nice when he nods and looks sorry for me.

Today I told Dr Robinson about the time I was sent home from school with a stomach ache and me and mum went to Harrods. She was getting mung beans or something from the food hall. On our way there, we were in the car, sitting at a set of traffic lights, somewhere around Hyde Park, listening to the car radio. The programme was one of those phone-in advice shows where people call in with medical problems. The radio doctor had this horrible way of talking – using baby words instead of the proper ones. 'And are there pains in *your tummy?' he would say. Or, 'Do you still feel icky in the mornings?' I was staying very quiet, hoping mum wouldn't suddenly remember that I was in the car and that the programme was unsuitable. Then Mum made a sound as if she had been hurt. Like 'Ouf'. I looked up at her and then followed where she was looking to the cab next to us. A man and woman were kissing. I felt that ticklish feeling, a sort of wanting to go to the loo, that I used to get when something sexy came on TV. It was a nice black shiny taxi making that fat, humming taxi noise and the woman, you couldn't see her because she had her back to us, dressed in something shimmery silver. I was thinking, No one wears that sort of thing in real life! Her legs were lying across the man's lap, and her arms were round his neck, like a lady in a film being rescued from the sea. The man's pale blue shirt. He had greying hair, too long at the back so it turned up in curls over his collar. Grey flannel trousers. And big black shoes. The ones I had polished the day before for 15p. The doctor on the radio was telling a joke. And mum's face got all big and scary, so close to me I could see her pores. A tear hanging from her chin like an icicle. Is thatdaddymummy? I said. Isthat daddymummy?mummymummy?*

Old Robbo was v. impressed. 'That must have been very difficult for you,' he said when I was done. They always say stuff like that. 'This must hurt.' Or, 'It's very hard to express your anger about this, isn't it?' Yeah, yeah, boo hoo.

Successful sexual congress following a bout of impotence is a wonderful thing. After I had come, Karen continued for a short while – changing her stroke in her efficient way to achieve her own orgasm. I watched her expression grow hard and unpretty with concentration. Shortly after that, I fell asleep. When I woke two hours or so later, stretched out jaggedly like a TV homicide on my damp, sex-dishevelled bed, Richard was knocking at the door, telling me that Karen had gone back to LA. I called him in to clarify. Karen had left an hour ago, he said. Penny had volunteered to drive her to the airport. I lay absorbing this information for a moment, while Richard offered some smutty speculations on whether or not I had managed to solicit 'a farewell fuck'. By rights, I should, I suppose, have been in a rather bad and guilty temper. But actually I was in excellent spirits. That thing about *omne* animal being *triste* after fucking has never rung a bell with me. On the contrary, the sex act tends to leave me feeling pretty cheerful. (Which is just as well, given how bloody *triste* I am the rest of the time.)

'What's Heidi doing?' I asked. Heidi was in the pool, Richard said. (Doing laps, naturally.) Presently, a slamming car door out in the street heralded Penny's return. Richard and I listened as she entered the house and began to trot about downstairs, tapping out victory with her heels.

'The girls were talking about going to the beach,' Richard said. 'Will you be joining us?'

I shook my head. 'I really should stay and do some work.'

Richard shrugged. 'Sure.' He hesitated, still hoping for some guy-talk. I hung tough.

'Well,' he said, 'I guess I'll go down and round up the girls then.'

Soon afterwards, Penny came clattering up to my room. She was trying not to look too gloating as she entered, but she couldn't help herself – she had the gleam and gait of a conquering valkyrie.

'Are you really not going to come?' she asked. I nodded.

'Ohwa!' she cried in a sulky little girl-voice. Then she came over and kissed me. I reared back slightly, fearful that the bedclothes and I smelled of sex. But she didn't seem to notice – either the smell or the flinch. Standing up straight, she pulled up her dress to reveal a rather ugly, crocheted bikini constructed out of tiny triangles of gilded wool and held together by what looked like curtain rings. 'Do you like it?' she asked.

'Yes!' I said.

'Do you think it's all right for me to go topless?' she asked.

I shook my head. 'No. I don't think so.'

I disapprove of topless sunbathing. I hate having that fried-egg stare of a woman's naked torso around me all day. In any case, the Mexicans don't like it.

'Aww, Willy,' Penny crooned. 'I'll get strap marks.'

'For Christ's sake!' I barked. 'You asked me and I'm telling you. You'll offend people. Not everybody is crazy to see your tits, you know.' Penny was silent. I saw a pinkness rise up her throat as she bent down, pretending to brush something from her leg.

No, no. Don't be a shit. Enough of that for one day. 'Anyway,' I added in a kinder tone, 'I like the strap marks. They're sexy.'

Penny smiled. God, she is easy to please. 'Willy!' she said. 'You *per*vert!' And God, I hate it when she calls me a pervert in that hopeful way.

'I'm just going to go downstairs and put some sodas in the cooler,' she announced now. At the door, she turned to look at me. 'Baby-cakes,' she said with a smile. 'I just want to say: don't go getting all guilty and freaked-out about the thing with that girl. As far as I'm concerned, it's over.'

I nodded, embarrassed.

For no obvious reason, she laughed then. 'Okay, big guy. I'm gonna love you and leave you – I don't want to miss the rays!' Then she shut the door.

With any woman other than Penny, I would take this 'no problem' speech as a mere postponement of the inevitable storm. Oona was a great one for hording damaging information with a cheery smile – carefully budgeting her resentments for the rainy days when she would blow everything on one great spree of righteousness. You would be cruising along, thinking that everything on the home front was basically under control, and then, one night over dinner, she'd start simmering. Her voice would take on a hushed viciousness. Her chin would begin to jut. Strange, angry patches of pink, like hickeys, would appear on her neck. She'd start off with some cool, bantering unpleasantness – witty little digs that a less experienced audience might have mistaken for jovial wifeliness. Then she would explode into earnest, sputtering rage and open up her ledger of my ancient offences and never-to-be-forgiven trespasses.

But not Penny. When she says, 'It's over', she means it. I suppose there is something a bit sicko about her reaction to the events of the last twenty-four hours. I don't know. I can see how some people would regard her behaviour as indicating a lack of dignity, or pride, or whatever. Penny's yenta girlfriends are always telling her she has a self-esteem problem. But maybe Penny's behaviour indicates the exact opposite. Maybe it shows a lot of pride and dignity. Most women in Penny's position would take the fact of my infidelity as some sort of personal insult. They'd yell and blub and yammer on about what it meant for Our Relationship. They'd pressure me into describing every little detail about the other woman, including the way she fucked. Then they'd get me to pretend that I hadn't really found her attractive at all and only fucked her because I was 'confused'. They'd threaten to leave but wouldn't. They'd go on bitching and moaning about it for at least two or three months, and, at the end of it all, they would be in exactly the same position as Penny is now. Only they would have exercised a lot more hormones getting there.

9

23 January 1978

*I have been living in Sophie's squat for two weeks. Aunt
Margaret says it is my life and if I want to ruin it there is
nothing she can do. Blah blah, old moo. Aunt Monika
was sweet and gave me some towels. It is not that nice
here. I like playing with Jack but the bath is slimey and
you have to walk for ages to get to a phone box and the
people in the shops give you dirty looks. Nial says its an
excellent squat, a lot better than ones he's been in. I have
a horrible spot on my chin – one of those ones that sits
cooking under your skin for about five weeks. This
morning when I took sophie a cup of tea in bed she
looked at me and said, I think that thing on your face is a
boil. And then she yelled at me for touching it.*

*Everyone else here is older than me and quite
condescending. All they do is take drugs. Nial is horrible.
He spends all day lying around on the floor under a dirty
old duvet complaining about things. He is always in a
bad mood and he treats me as if I was five years old. He
says I am a spoilt little rich girl. He has got a big chip on
his shoulder because his dad worked in a factory once. If
I am spoilt then sophie is too but he never says it about
sophie. Sometimes, if he's in a good mood, he'll talk to
me and tell me I am quite perceptive, but when people
say that all they mean is that you have the same
perceptions as them. He has these freak-outs when he has
taken too many different drugs. The doctor told him they
are 'toxic confusions'. He starts to giggle and talk*

rubbish and cry and pick at himself. I spend a lot of time in my room so I don't have to talk to him. I have got a job at a beauty salon place, they call it a spa, in Knightsbridge. It is just at reception, but the woman who runs it, Anita, says she might arrange for me to go on a training course to learn how to do some of the treatments. I have to deal with some right old bags and the money is crap, but at least I can sit down and the other girls are quite a laugh. Nial and Sophie say it is exploitation and I am a mug.

Sophie looks tired all the time because Jack is such a handful. She is still very pretty though and all the men in the house want to sleep with her. I try to imagine what her life is like, but I can't really. She is always talking about sex. She has been to bed with loads of people. The other day, she told me that when we lived in Leeds, she had it off with Uncle Bill. She says they did it in the car the first week we were there when they went on a shopping trip to buy cagoules.

Today we went shopping in the covered market in the town centre. Within half an hour, Penny had purchased a hundred dollars-worth of candy skulls and corn dollies and folk bracelets made out of coloured string. Then she came across a mirror – one of those big things framed with elaborately indented tin. She liked it, but wasn't sure that she ought to: a typical Penny dilemma. She wanted me to arbitrate – *Oh Willy, do you think it's cute?* – but I couldn't help. I don't know whether a Mexican tin mirror is a good thing or not. I'm just like her – looking to be told. Eventually she had to fetch Heidi, who was over at the fruit stalls, and bring her back to give her judgement. Heidi knew right away, of course. The mirror was an ugly piece of tat that would be exceptionally cumbersome to transport all the way to Los Angeles. Ethnic was tired, she said. Heidi is one of those people who always know these things. She and her friends swim along together, like beautiful pilot fish, intuiting, with perfect and mysterious synchronicity, which abrupt change of fashion direction they are next going to take. People like Penny and me float about on the brilliant periphery of these information centres, hoping for guidance. But however hard we try, we are destined to be at least one or two fatal moves behind. I don't aspire to be fashionable. To be in possession of a coherent, identifiable look would be quite enough. I have been plunging hopefully into new 'lifestyles' all my adult life – convinced each time I do so that at last I have found my stylistic home. Oh, the things I have tried out! The polo shirts with designer logos, the American colonial quilts, the parquet flooring, the Zapata moustaches, the Captain Haddock beards! The bright silk shirts with flapping collars, the black silk sheets, the cowboy boots, the Mies van der Rohe leather chairs, the French antiques, the art deco posters, the marble tiled bathrooms, the Italian country tiled kitchens, the tweed jackets with leather elbow patches. The braces, the vintage kipper ties, the American loafers, the English brogues, the Dunhill lighters, the hand-knitted fisherman's sweaters, the executive toys in chrome and black leather, the massage chairs, the incense, the cologne, the nineteenth-century water-colours, the twentieth-century lithographs, the signet rings. Time and again I have spent fortunes acquiring all the accoutrements of a new guise, only to cast it off after a month or so when I catch my clownish reflection in a shop window or see a photograph of myself. I am not to be trusted.

It was an important part of Oona's allure when I first met her – her clear and unwavering views on matters of style. She wasn't fashionable, like Heidi. On the contrary, she was always slightly tatty to look at. But she had an absolute faith in her own judgements: so much so that she didn't really perceive them as judgements at all, just simple matters of fact. I was a disapproving young man when I met her. I wrote poetry about coal miners and the class struggle and made jokes about tainting Oona's smug English genealogy with my sickly mittel-European blood. I pretended to abhor her upper middle classness. But in truth, I was covetous. Oona had gone to Oxford, where she had run the Labour club and done something important at the Union and won the Herbert FuckFace Memorial prize for an essay on David Hume. She was a big one for pointing out the logical errors – the 'woolly' thinking – in other people's arguments. Someone once said to Oona, 'You think too much,' and I saw her flush with pride. She was meant to end up running the BBC or being the Director of Public Prosecutions or something. (She didn't, of course. She married me and had two kids and did a bunch of pissy little jobs for the Labour Party. But neither of us knew that then.) She spent her summers at her parents' house in the Orkneys, where everyone drank whisky from antique flasks and read interesting things from the newspaper to one another over breakfast and took very few baths because of the defective boiler. With Oona, I imagined, I might finally muscle my way into the secret garden of Englishness. I was enthralled by her – by her enormous swimmer's shoulders and the odd, angry little flick she gave her hair, and how she pronounced certain words in ways I had never heard before ('bee-zar' for 'bizarre' and 'becourse' for 'because'). Even her obscenities – 'Fuckaduck', 'Bloody bollocks' – seemed exotic to me. Later, when I got to know her friends, I found they all spoke that way – but, being in love, I didn't think to reassess my first impression of her supreme originality. I simply assumed that her friends were imitating her.

Early on in our courtship, she took me to meet her parents at their home – a subsiding Georgian townhouse on a dark, mossy lane in Hampstead. They maintained the place in a state of scrupulous squalor. Spidery fissures crept across the high ceilings; the main staircase was in the process of coming away from the wall and the stench of cat piss was everywhere – rising off the furniture like steam from a kettle. I was repulsed but awestruck. Their walls were painted terracotta and covered with unframed paintings by artists *they knew*. At last, English bohemia!

Her father, Paul, who met us at the door ('Hellohellohellohello!'), was grey-haired and gangly in a moth-eaten corduroy jacket and baggy old man's pants. He had the scent of jumble sale about him – ripe wool and old sweat – and, to my utter horror, he greeted Oona by kissing her on the lips. In the living room (dark, stinky, book-lined) Sibella was bending down to feed a great squad of yowling cats. She was flushed and fat and she wore a big, peasant-style dress that looked as if it had been blown on to her by chance during a violent storm. Her long hair hung in greasy, yellow-white hanks about her pudding-face. Every time she smiled, she offered a glimpse of a truly terrifying dental landscape – dank and mulchy with glittering pockets of gold filling. It was marvellous to me that a beauty of Oona's stature should have sprung from the loins of such an old potato.

For dinner, or 'supper' as they called it, there was no starter, just stew – the fancy, Elizabeth David kind, with bits of dried apricot in it. There was red wine in pyrex tumblers that Sibella boasted she'd bought with Green Shield Stamps. And when I was done with my first helping, she scraped at the gluey mess in the bottom of the stew-pot and held it out on a wooden spoon for me. 'Willy – you'll have some of the gubbins, won't you?'

Going home afterwards, I was in a terrible temper. I teased Oona about her parents – imitating their accents and accusing them of condescension. 'Oh Hellehhh!

Hellehhh you mahvellous little Jewy Jew! How fascinating to meet you!' I shouted, capering grotesquely about the underground station platform.

'But they're *not* like that,' Oona objected. 'And they liked you very much. I could tell.'

'Oh, how *nice* of them. How open-minded. They are wonderfully accepting up here in Hampstead, aren't they? I dare say Mummy will give you a call tomorrow – "Darling, what a lovely little Jewy Jew you brought to supper. We must get him together with some of our other Jewy chums."'

Oona didn't bother to reply. She just walked away – left me on the station platform and caught a bus home.

They *had* been kind to me – leaning in close across the dinner table to catch my whispered contributions to the conversation, nodding furiously whenever I said anything they could actually hear. Me! This monosyllabic know-nothing, shtupping their best girl! They had wanted to know all about my childhood in Germany. But I had been offended by their interest. Their graciousness made me feel awkward and ashamed. I didn't want to be an interesting refugee. I didn't want to be foreign. I wanted to be noise-lessly, smoothly absorbed into things.

After Penny had been persuaded out of buying the mirror, we went home and the others spent the afternoon by the pool, while I went into the living room to work. No doubt it's the stress of the last twenty-four hours, but after about ten minutes of lolling at Sissy Yerxa's bureau, I found myself falling asleep. I roused myself, made a cup of coffee. Then, I really went off the deep end and took it into my head to write to Sophie. Christ. Next thing you know, I'm going to be running about naked on a storm-swept heath.

'*Dear Sophie,*' I wrote, '*I bet you didn't expect to hear from your old Dad!*' I stopped here and considered the exclamation mark. Then, with a mad sort of abruptness, I tore off the sheet of paper and screwed it up. In preparation for the letter, I had compiled a brief list of Topics To Cover, which I now consulted.

1. heart attack.
2. haven't seen you in a long time.
3. how are you?
4. Sadie and/or Oona. (Poignant memory???)
5. the journals.
6. let bygones be bygones. Suggest visit.
7. weather, love, etcetera.

'*Dear Sophie,*' I started again,

'*In case you were ever thinking of having one, I should tell you now, heart attacks aren't a lot of fun.*'

Yikes – what was with that Hail Fellow irony? Another start.

'*Dear Sophie,*

How are you? As you know, I have not been well, but now I seem to be on the mend.'

On the mend?

'*Dear Sophie,*

I know you must be quite busy at the moment, but it would be lovely if you came to see me one of these days.'

Good, good. Cutting to the chase.

'*You would enjoy the weather here and I would be very . . .*'

Uh oh. Might the invitation not suggest a willingness on my part to pay her airfare?

'*I understand that you can get some quite good deals on standby flights.*'

A quick look back at the checklist.

'*You and Sadie have been in my thoughts a lot recently. Just before I got ill, I received a parcel of Sadie's old journals that she must have sent me shortly before . . .*'

Well, obviously, this was a crazy project. I tore up all my abortive attempts and put them in the bin. Clearly my daughter Sophie does not want to hear from me, and frankly, I – when I am not getting carried away by the pubescent mawkishness of Sadie – do not want to hear from her. I honestly don't know what's gotten into me. I must see if I have any Valium in my medicine bag.

IO

17 June 1978

Am feeling v. v. depressed. Sophie and Nial and Jack are
finally going to get a council flat. I am happy for them
and glad to get rid of Nial but I don't want to stay in the
squat on my own. Everyone is so horrid here apart from
Lydia, and even she is quite condescending sometimes. I
don't have any real friends. It isn't that safe here either.
The other day marcus the man downstairs came back
and found a tramp in his room.

I told Sophie I would miss her and Jack and she got
really bitchy and said I was just doing my Little Nell. She
is awful at the moment – always arguing with Nial and
hitting Jack.

Today a man came in to work – a foreign man, said he
wanted a massage. I said I'm sorry sir, but I think you've
made a mistake – this is a women only beauty salon. He
got really mad and started shouting at me. The girls were
wetting themselves. I tried to explain again, very slowly
and politely but he shouted, You dont know sixpence!
You think I'm stupid! You don't know sixpence, you
stupid little whore! Anita had to throw him out.
Afterwards, everyone referred to me affectionately, all
day, as 'the stupid little whore'. I really wish I had a
boyfriend.

I am feeling very, very tired. Richard and Heidi finally left
for LA on Tuesday. Twenty-four hours later (i.e. yesterday)
my friend Harry arrived from England. Most of this morn-

ing has been spent supervising the clean-up operation required after his first night's tequila-sodden debauches. The minute I spotted him from the airport viewing-deck yesterday afternoon – a vibrantly pink dot, weaving his way down the plane steps – I could tell he was drunk. He doesn't like to admit it, but Harry is petrified of flying. He had been drinking vodka all the way from London. Having managed to fold his enormous 6'4" frame into the rental jeep, he immediately produced two miniatures from his trouser pockets and gulped them both down in rapid succession. He then gave a loud fart and passed out.

I had assumed he would be out of action for the rest of the night, but at around seven he rallied dramatically and came roaring downstairs from his bedroom, demanding to be entertained. I ended up taking him and Penny to one of the cheesier American hang-outs in town – a place called the Coconut Cabana, where Harry consumed a large plate of steak and chips (he didn't like the look of the Mexican muck) and was ebulliently offensive to everyone in sight. For reasons to do with sentimentality and auld lang syne, I am largely protected from Harry's alcoholic spite. But Penny receives no such exemption. Most of his jibes went over her head, but her first impression was unfavourable, nevertheless. Penny is quite happy to put up with bad behaviour from rich or famous people – licence to behave boorishly is the *point* of being rich and famous as far as she is concerned – but Harry's coarseness, unjustified by money or celebrity, violates her profoundest sense of the order of things. 'He's so *tacky*,' she said, more in wonderment than in anger, at one point during the evening, when he had staggered off to the loo.

There is no denying that Harry does cut a rather repulsive figure these days, but it is still startling to hear someone say so. When I first met Harry, he was more or less irresistible to women. They actually used to drop their handkerchieves in order to attract his attention. This was 1951. We were both fresh out of National Service, working as cub reporters for the *Hendon Herald*. (Harry had done his time in Germany, working as an intelligence officer; I had spent three years down the mines in Dunfermline, conscientiously objecting.) The pickings for a junior reporter in 1950s Hendon were not good. Our beat consisted almost entirely of weddings, funerals, kittens in trees and the occasional house fire. Harry was very unserious about work – always late for his shift, always behind on his deadlines – but in spite of this he was generally considered to be the best man on the paper. I regarded him with pained, resentful awe. He was the tallest and the poshest person I had ever come into close contact with. He was also my first exposure to authentic charm. Something about his breezy, unkempt presence made people go soft. It wasn't just that they liked him; they wanted him to like *them*. They fell over themselves to show him their bank records, their love letters, their underwear drawers. He never had to bark questions as the other reporters did. He just stood and gazed and waited for his lanky charisma to take its effect. 'Yah . . . Coo! . . . Yah . . . Gosh, really?' he would mutter sweetly, as the apples fell into his lap. It was Harry who got the Mayor of Hendon's wife to confess that she didn't much care for 'wogs'.

He never bothered to learn shorthand. He wrote entirely from memory (with a little help from his imagination). Sometimes, the editor would demand evidence to back up his more baroque or outrageous quotes, and on these occasions Harry would ferret out an old envelope covered in squiggles and pictograms that he kept in his desk drawer expressly for the purpose. 'There,' he would say, in a hurt tone, as he whisked it under the editor's nose. 'Can I go now?' I was always expecting – wanting – his poshness to alienate his co-workers, but it never did. All the girls in the office were in love with him. He would sit on their desks in his expensive, egg-stained shirts and scuffed Bond Street brogues, reciting poetry to them in his fruity voice, while they fiddled with their hair and gazed up at him longingly.

When I first met Oona, I held off, for several months, from introducing her to Harry, convinced that once Harry did his number on her she would think of me as shoddy goods. When they finally met, however, Harry took against her on sight. 'She'll have your balls on her key-chain in no time,' he told me. He was never rude to her. On the contrary, he expressed his hostility by being elaborately formal and polite – 'Would your lady-friend care for another beverage, Willy?' – with the happy result that Oona considered him socially inept and rather dull. 'He's a nice enough little insect,' she told me airily. 'But a bit of a bore. Why are you so attached to him?'

To no one's surprise, Harry's career in journalism began and ended at the *Herald*. He left after a year to try his hand at banking, and when that failed he had a go at studying law. Finally, he fell, with infallible posh-person's luck, into acting. He was not particularly talented, but he had a good face for movies, and during the sixties he had quite a bit of success, playing a series of ruddy-complexioned toffs in Hollywood war pictures. For several years I didn't see much of him. Then, when Oona died, he re-entered my life. Harry never asked me about Oona's death. Never once demanded to know what 'really' happened. Having aided me in my botched escape attempt, he was – apart from Monika – the only person to visit me with any regularity in prison. And after I came out he went to terrific lengths to help me fend off depression. His movie career had started to go downhill by this point. He was living in a smelly bedsit in Belsize Park, doing bits and pieces of theatre and the odd BBC play but mostly hanging around in pubs and betting clubs. He had begun to develop the porous-looking pink nose of a professional boozer. His friends were all drinking friends – ruined-faced geezers who referred to each other by affectionately obscene names and kept their wives in purdah in Essex. All of which was a great comfort to me, at that difficult stage in my life.

When we got back from the Cabana last night, Harry raged about the house for a while, managing, in the process, to spill a full ashtray into the swimming pool and pour red wine on to Sissy Yerxa's white rug. Eventually he fell into a drunken swoon on the sofa with a lit cigar in his fat hand. He woke briefly as Penny and I were dragging him upstairs and expressed his desire to give someone (or something) 'a good rogering'. In his room, we got his shoes off and levered him on to the bed. And then, as we were leaving, he surfaced into semi-consciousness once more. 'Where are the wenches?' he was calling plaintively into the darkness as I closed the door.

During the night, he crowned his achievements by copiously wetting his bed. I know this because this morning, as he was lying out on the veranda sucking up a pint of Bloody Mary, the maid called me in to his room to witness the befoulment of her snowy linens.

Harry is clearly going to be a difficult guest.

II

1 July 1978

*Sophie and Nial have moved out now. I have tonsilitis
and Marcus who lives downstairs shouted at me today
because I drank some of his milk. He called me a
screw-faced bitch. I went to the doctor's for antibiotics
and when he asked me how I was feeling in myself, I
burst into tears. He told me I was run down. I took the
bus home. A nutty woman got on at The Strand wearing
a paper crown like the ones you get out of a cracker. At
one point, the bus took a sharp corner, and her crown
came apart. She took it off and handed it to the Indian
woman sitting next to her and the woman proceeded
very gamely to mend it for her and give it back.*

*Lydia took me to a party on the weekend. I met a
bloke called Adam, who said he was a writer, but it turns
out he's just an assistant to an editor at Bunty or
something. We went back to his house in Crouch End
with some other people and we all ended up staying. I
am always so stupid and shy in those situations. I don't
know what to say to people and I feel so stupid and ugly
and young. In the middle of the night, Adam woke me
and asked me to go upstairs with him. He had a bong.
He wasn't at all good-looking but I was flattered. He got
quite stoned. Then he kissed me. His breath had a weird
salami taste and his mouth was sticky like a licked
postage stamp and it left a residue of slime around my
mouth. Then he put his hands down my jeans and poked
at me a bit. After about three minutes, he told me to take*

my clothes off, so I did. I said did he have condoms and
he said don't worry I'll be careful. It wasn't as scary as I
thought it would be. It was over very fast and I didn't
bleed thank God. I must have been quite convincing
because afterwards he said I was polymorphosly (???)
perverted and when I asked what does that mean? he said
it means you like everything. I couldn't believe how hairy
his bum was. Afterwards he said it would be better if I
went back downstairs to sleep because it wouldn't be
cool if everyone knew, so I went back down. We left
really early in the morning and on the bus back Lydia
said, 'That bloke Adam, talk about desperate – he was
trying it on with everyone.'

Yesterday we went to the beach, Harry, Penny and I. Penny
spent most of the time skipping about in the frothy tide,
making a great show of wistful shell-collecting. Harry tied
a handkerchief on his head and played the yobbish Englishman *en vacances*. All very tiresome – but marginally less
screechy on the nerves than being holed up with the two
of them at Casa De La Bumfuck. Penny is on my case all
the time about smoking (giving it up) and sex (having it)
and Harry (getting rid of him). Harry bangs on about any
manner of nonsensical, drunken shit for hours on end and
grows offended if his capering isn't given a rapt audience.
The other day, I had a brilliant idea for shutting him up: I
bet him a hundred bucks that he couldn't read the Bible
straight through in ten days. He took the bet, but unfortu-
nately it has had no effect on his constant chatter, other
than to inject it with a new, gruesomely religioso flavour.
He lies moistly on the sofa, tutting and clucking over Sissy
Yerxa's King James Version, looking up every two minutes
to pass inane comment: 'Fucking hell, Willy, did you know
that the bit about physicians healing themselves comes in
the Bible?' Or, more simply, 'God, God is a shit, isn't he?'

When it becomes clear that I am not listening, he starts to bait Penny. For the most part, she has been content to swish about with raised eyebrows, pretending not to hear his insults. But the other evening, when Harry referred to her as 'a pointless fucking wench', she threw a glass at him and demanded that I do something to defend her honour.

Naturally, I did no such thing. I crept away to bed, leaving them to burble and whimper at each other in their respectively crapulent and tear-sodden ways. Sooner or later I am going to have to do something about this situation.

In the afternoon, I did a little work and took a nap. I woke to the sound of the phone ringing. It was Art.

'It's going great, Art,' I said, as soon as I heard his voice. 'I'm very excited about it.'

He sighed. 'It's all right, Willy,' he said. 'I'm not calling to hassle you. I'm calling you to let you know that Hans Stempel is vacationing about ten miles from you. He's got a house out there.'

'Get out.'

'Really. And guess what? Sissy Yerxa told him you were renting her place. He's going to be calling you.'

'Wait a minute, I thought I was meant to be in hiding.'

'You're meant to be in retreat.'

'Yeah, but I thought the idea was to keep me away from everybody so no one would know I'd been sick.'

'Right. So, for God's sake, if you see him, make sure you're looking good.'

'Why would I want to see him?'

'Willy, don't be an asshole about this. If he calls, be nice, okay?'

About ten minutes after I hung up on Art, Stempel called.

'Hi! Is that Villy Muller? Oh, great! This is Hans Stempel! I just found out yesterday that we are neighbours! Welcome to Pee Vee!'

'Thanks.'

'First of all, Villy, let me say, I love your book and I think we're going to make a super movie together!'

There was a pause here, which, according to the rules of such exchanges, I should have filled with some blushing statement of my unworthiness. Naturally, I stayed absolutely silent.

'So, now secondly, Villy,' he went on. (Surprised you there, didn't I, Krauty?) 'I am having a party for my girl-friend's birthday tonight, and I was wondering if perhaps you would like to come!'

Normally, I would rather stick pins in my eyes than accept the hospitality of a man like Stempel, but given my alternative – another night of Harry and Penny duking it out over backgammon – I said yes. He proceeded to give me five minutes of incredibly detailed instructions on how to get to his house. 'And then you turn into a liddle, liddle road – it's about the size of my prick. Her, her, her! Just before you get to the, uh, helmet, you turn left . . .'

What a moron.

Judging by the way they responded to the Stempel invi-tation, I have to assume that Harry and Penny are just as sick to death of this Mexican idyll as I am. Both of them behaved like castaways catching sight of a passing cruise liner. Penny became breathless with excitement and immediately darted into the bathroom to start readying herself, even though it was only three o'clock and the party wasn't starting until seven. Harry made a great pretence of being outraged at the idea of accepting hospitality from a German ('Damn it, Willy, I can't drink a Hun's booze – the stuff would choke me!') But about an hour later, when I passed his bedroom, I caught a glimpse of him brushing his tongue, which I correctly took to mean that he had changed his mind.

I went to the living room and tried doing some more

work, but my concentration wasn't good. It was an odd sensation, being in a household of people preparing themselves for an evening out. My life doesn't have many of these cosy, communal moments any more. In the old days, with Oona and the girls, there were a lot of group outings – circuses and ice-skating shows and birthday suppers – nights when the house would be filled with the buzz and squabble of three females making their toilettes: Oona brushing her hair with strict, strenuous strokes, as if she was angry with it, Sadie pleading to be allowed to wear glittery make-up on her eyes, Sophie deflecting objections to her unsuitable fuck-me costumes with attacks on the way I was dressed. '*Daaad, you can't go out like that . . .*'

If I'm honest, I would have to say that most of the time I spent as a fully paid-up father, I slightly resented my kids. Well, not them so much, but their attitude – their idiotic happiness about things – the way they saw their life as this orderly progression of school days and holidays, presents and punishments. They had such cheery confidence in the pleasures that the world had to offer. I suppose what I'm saying is that I resented their innocence. They *were* innocent – even Sophie. They hadn't been beaten down; they weren't scared yet. It bugged me. But sometimes, on those treat nights, I didn't mind the innocence so much. In fact, I actually liked it. For a short time, I could get caught up in their way of seeing. I could believe that life *was* this spangly carousel of bonfire nights and Madame Tussaud's and squabbles with Fatty Jenkins in the school playground.

We set off at six forty-five, calculating that it would take around twenty minutes to get to Stempel's. Harry had put on a blazer. Penny was overdressed in a cocktail dress made out of some odd, greyish-orange velvet. She looked like a rotting peach. Stempel lives on an expensively remote part of the coast, where the roads give way to a maze of dirt-tracks. In spite of the instructions, I managed to get us lost. It was a stressful journey, throughout which Harry pointedly sang and re-sang 'We're Going to Hang Our Washing on the Siegfried Line', and Penny, who had been forced to forsake the girlfriend's front-seat prerogative because Harry is too large to fit in the rear, breathed hot resentment on the back of my neck. By the time we arrived, I was ready for a dark room and a cold compress.

Stempel's house – which is called Casa De La Warrior in a cute reference to the movie that paid for it – sits at the end of a half-mile driveway, right on the beach. It's a very recent construction and uncommonly large for properties in this area: a money-house. Directors, no matter how slim their talent, or how marginal their success, always seem to be rolling in it. Last year, I went to a party in Beverly Hills held by this malignant dwarf called Eric Begelmann. The most important thing Begelmann has ever done is a cop caper – sorry, no, a cop caper *sequel* – called *Piggies II*, but he lives in a glass and maplewood palace with a swimming pool, some kind of cockamaimie conservatory extension and a 21-year-old brunette who wears a baseball cap embroidered with the words, 'The Big Begel'. Tuh.

Stempel's party was in full swing when we arrived, which is to say about twenty Pee Vee locals – elderly American expatriates, mostly – were gathered on the veranda, making free with the guacamole dip. Down on the beach, a rather dejected little Mariachi band was playing Mexican songs of love. The first person to greet us was Sissy Yerxa, looking like a lipsticked ferret in a very short skirt and an electric pink halter-neck.

'Hiiii!' she wailed. 'Willy! Good to see you!'

I kissed her proffered cheek. 'Harry, Penny, this is Sissy Yerxa, our landlady.'

'Oh don't call me that!' Sissy shrieked, spearing my ribs with her elbow. 'Hi guys! I hope you're enjoying Casa De La Luna.'

Harry made noises of assent. Penny put out her hand to shake. 'Oh, Sissy! I've been dying to meet you!' she said. Sissy is one of those rich women who pride themselves on being tremendously unaffected and down to earth. But she tends to get scratchy when the little people whom she is polite enough to pretend are her equals do not show themselves sufficiently sensible of the condescension. She gave Penny a flinty once-over while allowing her limp hand to be shaken. Then she turned to Harry.

'You're so tall!' she exclaimed, batting him coquettishly on the chest.

'Isn't he?' Penny agreed.

Sissy ignored her. 'How did you get to be so tall?'

Harry muttered something unintelligible.

'I guess he ate a lot of spinach!' Penny said cheerfully.

Sissy turned to her now. 'You know, it's very odd,' she said, with regal slowness. 'You look quite different from the last time I saw you . . .'

'No, no, you haven't met Penny before,' I interrupted hastily. 'That was someone else you met . . .'

Sissy gave me a vulgar look. 'Oh, Willy, I can't keep up with your social schedule . . .' Penny's face seemed to melt.

'Hey,' Sissy said now, pointing to a tall, gaunt man who was approaching us, 'did you meet our host yet?'

'Heeey!' Stempel crowed, with the sort of nerve-jangling pseudo-delight that some people feel is required at festive occasions. 'Are you by any chance Villy? I'm Hans!'

He had a long arrow-nose and almost no lips – his mouth was just an unannounced slit in the final third of his face, like a muppet's. He was wearing pale green linen trousers and a collarless white linen shirt, with the sleeves rolled up. His eyes were an unlikely grass green. (Vanity contact lenses, I suspect.) Harry, I noticed, was humming, 'Who Do You Think You Are Kidding, Mr Hitler?' under his breath.

'I'm so glad you could come!' Stempel said, banging me on the back. Then he began speaking to me in German – something noxious about how nice it was to find a fellow countryman out here. I cut him off with a shake of my head. 'I'm not a German-speaker any more, I'm afraid.'

He rolled his eyes. 'Oh, Villy! That's terri-bul! We shall have to do something about that!'

He introduced the birthday girl, a simpering blonde called Brandy who was visiting him from LA for a couple of days. I introduced Penny and Harry. Then Stempel told Brandy to go fetch his children. (Harry, who regards anyone under thirty as mildly toxic, wandered off at this point to get a drink.) Brandy returned promptly, shepherding a surly boy of about ten and a rather beautiful little girl of five or six. The impression was of a game show's lady-assistant bringing forth two new contestants.

'This is Otto and Anna,' Stempel said, regarding the two of them sternly. 'They are normally living with their mother in Munich, but I have them for the summer holidays.'

He addressed himself to them now: '*Was sagt Ihr denn?*'

The boy and girl looked down at the floor and then off into the middle distance. 'How do you do?' they murmured dutifully, in turn.

Stempel rolled his eyes at us. 'I am trying to get them to learn some English. Perhaps you can help each other, Villy! You can coach them in English and they can refresh your German!'

Penny patted the boy gingerly on his head. Then she bent down and amiably prodded the little girl. Penny has never had children of her own and responds to other people's with the sort of disinterested admiration that one normally reserves for pets. 'Wow!' she said, looking up at Stempel. 'She's got amazing skin! You can't see a single pore on her!'

When he judged that the children had been sufficiently

praised, Stempel ordered Brandy to take them back to their au pair and have them put to bed. Obediently, woman and children removed themselves. 'Now, Villy,' Stempel said, putting a skinny arm around my shoulder. 'Let's get you and your lovely lady-friend a drink.' At the drinks table, Harry was instructing a Mexican youth on how to make a proper martini. Penny and I opted for red wine. (I drank one glass down immediately and took another.) Stempel ordered a Diet Coke. 'Villy, I must tell you that your script has really knocked me out,' he said while our drinks were being poured. 'I think it's an ebsolutely febulous story and you tell it really beautifully. I am so anxious to work with you on this project. I hope your little polish is going to be ready real soon ... Ah! Please, here is Raymond!' A shiny-faced man in an orange Mexican dress-shirt stepped forward and squeezed my hand. The heels on his patent leather shoes must have been at least three inches high. 'Villy, this is Raymond Brinks,' Stempel said. 'My decorating consultant on this place. The poor guy has been with me throughout this whole crazy project.'

Raymond raised his hands in outraged denial. '"Poor guy!" Are you kidding? I can't tell you what a fabulous time I've had working on this place. I mean, it's been a trip ...'

'Now, Villy!' Stempel shouted, growing bored with Raymond's enthusiasm. 'I would love it for you and Penny to come with Raymond and I on a tour of my house.'

I offered a strained, crocodile rictus. There was apparently no escape. 'I would love to. Penny?'

'*Ja!* Penny!' Stempel said. '*Ja!* You must come too!'

We all trooped up a wrought-iron spiral staircase just off the veranda, Stempel leading the way. 'Okay,' he said, on the first-floor landing. 'Here is my study.' He pushed open a door and led us into a very large, very dark room, done out in cherry wood and red velvet. 'Pretty amazing, huh?' he said. 'I like to feel as if I'm in the womb when I'm working.'

Just hearing this man say the word 'womb' makes you want to vomit.

On his huge oak desk there was a computer the approximate size of my rental jeep. 'What do you use, Villy?' Stempel asked. 'Are you a compuder person? *Ja?* Oh great! Well, then, you will love this. This is an amazing machine. I am todally in love with it!'

Adjoining the study was Stempel's library – stuffed with heavy, Krauty antiques. 'Raymond here is a world-renowned expert on eighteenth-century furniture,' Stempel said. 'And I think it would be correct to say, Raymond, you are freaked out by the items in this room?' Raymond shook his head to indicate how freaked out he was. After the library, there were some guest bedrooms in which we briefly glimpsed Otto watching satellite television and Anna being tucked in by a porky little German au pair.

Then there was 'the media room' – a miniature movie theatre, equipped with something called 'sub-woofers' – and, at the end of the hall, another guest suite, on whose walls a local artist, commissioned by Raymond, had painted a pink and green Mexican theme mural featuring lots of sombreros and sloe-eyed chicas.

'Villy, when you get back to L A you must come and visit me at my house,' Stempel said. 'Robert did the decoration on that, too. And I have a febulous liddle sauna – you and Penny must come take a sauna with me!' The phrase 'Fat chance' bubbled up to my lips and then receded. What is it with Krauts and saunas? Why are they all so mad keen for group nakedness and hot pine?

Stempel was now leading us to the second floor and the master bathroom – a long, narrow, high-ceilinged room, completely covered in tiny yellow and ochre tiles. There were two twin basins – one ochre, one yellow, with gilded faucets in the shape of dolphins – and, in the middle of the room, two vast, stone bath-tubs. Each bath had its own side-table equipped with a telephone and a small pile of books. 'Essentially,' Stempel said, 'we built this room around the baths. Febulous, huh? I found them in an antique shop just outside Florence and immediately I knew I had to have them. You see, they are positioned so we are getting a really terrific view from the window when we bathe. As you can imagine, Villy, I spend a lot of time in this room.'

Raymond started to say something here, about his inspiration for the colour scheme, but halfway through his little speech, Stempel turned away. He bent down and opened a tiled cabinet next to one of the basins, which turned out to be a refrigerator, filled with bottles of champagne. 'You like this?' he said, leering at Penny. 'It's pretty neat, no?'

I hadn't really been registering Penny's reactions until this moment, but glancing at her now I saw that, indeed, she did seem to think Stempel's place was pretty neat. Her eyes were glassy with longing, her mouth a tight little O of avarice. Stempel saw this too, and laughed. I had a quick look at his bath-time reading, before we left. On the top of one pile was a book called *Fetish*. On the other, *Justine*. Too much information, as the young people say.

Then there was the bedroom – white-walled and empty but for an outsize fourposter bed and an antique tapestry hanging over it. 'No distractions,' Stempel said, waving his arms at the emptiness. 'I think bedrooms are for sleeping and making love – nothing else. Do you agree, Villy?' Though the question was directed at me, he was looking at Penny, who responded, maddeningly enough, by blushing. *Okay, flirt with the Marquis De Nazi, then, you old slapper. Let's see how you like it when he brings out the hot wax and the nipple clamps.*

By the time we had returned to the ground floor and seen

the slate and granite kitchen, the Jim Dine in the living room and the collection of naughty postcards in the powder room, Stempel's little tour had lasted almost half an hour. Released back on to the veranda, I could see that Harry was half-cut. He was talking in a highly animated fashion to Brandy, and as I passed by I distinctly overheard him saying something about the '*Luftwaffe*'. I went to the drinks table and drank down a couple more glasses of red wine, before scurrying away to avoid the approach of Sissy Yerxa.

Stempel now declared that there was to be dancing and ordered the band to provide some 'up-tempo' numbers. Fairly soon the veranda was filled with couples whirling about to Mariachi renditions of 'You are the Sunshine of My Life' and 'Mrs Robinson'. Harry danced with Brandy. Stempel danced with Penny. I stood and watched. If you set aside Stempel's revolting exclamations ('All *right!* Woooh!'), you would have to judge him a pretty good dancer. Penny was obviously getting a big kick out of the experience. She had that glinty-eyed, wet-lipped look about her. From a distance, the rotting-peach dress seemed not quite so eccentric. She looked pretty cute, even. For one insane second, as I watched her and Stempel loom in and out of the dancing crowd, I felt a twinge of jealousy.

I wandered inside to take a pee. Passing the kitchen, I saw Stempel's little girl sitting at the counter with the au pair. They were eating cookies and talking softly together. They looked up now and saw me. 'Hello,' the girl said. Her voice had a pretty, sing-song quality. I nodded back in greeting.

'I should be in bed,' she said in German. 'But I needed some cookies.'

I nodded again and smiled, wondering how to get away.

'Would you like a cookie?' she asked. The au pair giggled. I shook my head.

'Don't you like cookies?' She leaned over the counter at

me, like some dwarfish talk-show host. Her nose was a tiny, squashy mushroom. Under the kitchen's strip-lighting, her pale blonde hair looked almost white.

I paused. 'What sort are they?' I asked. After so long, the German words sounded odd and unwieldy in my mouth.

'*Zimsterne*,' she said, holding up one of the star-shaped cookies.

'Oh, well, in that case, I would like one, please. I haven't had *Zimsterne* since I was a very little boy.' A memory swam into my head of my mother telling me, aged nineteen, that I spoke German like a pig.

The girl looked at me, trying to weigh up if I really wanted one or was just being cute. 'Okay,' she said. I came forward to take the cookie from her outstretched hand. She and the au pair watched me expectantly as I ate it.

'Hmm!' I said, after I had theatrically swallowed. 'That was delicious! Thank you!'

The little girl shrugged. '*Zimsterne* are my favourite cookies.'

I stared at her. She really was a startlingly pretty girl. She cocked her head and stared back, her white-blonde eyebrows forming sceptical arcs.

'I have to go now,' I said. 'But thank you very much for the cookie. It was nice of you to give me one.'

'That's all right,' she said, smiling magnanimously. 'Goodbye.'

A few moments later, as I stood over Stempel's toilet bowl, staring at his stupid fucking postcards, I had the bizarre sensation of being about to cry.

We got lost again on the journey home. By the time we had got unlost and were staggering up Sissy Yerxa's driveway, it was almost midnight. Penny went straight to bed. Harry and I sat out on the veranda for a while, drinking Grand Marnier nightcaps.

'You know, Harry,' I said, after a long, drinking silence,

'before she died, Sadie sent me these journals of hers. It's very odd – I've been reading them and . . .' I paused.

Harry was gazing at me fixedly. I couldn't tell whether he was concentrating on what I was saying or about to pass out.

'Yes?' he said, after a while.

'Well, obviously they're pretty rough reading.'

Harry grunted.

'I . . . I must say, it's been very sobering for me. You know, it's made me think a lot about the past and . . . and so on.'

This attempt at intimacy was a terrible mistake on my part, I realized. Harry was fidgeting wildly now, fighting a losing battle against looking aghast.

'Anyway, how about another drink?' I said, picking up the bottle.

Harry stared down at his feet while I poured, and murmured something inaudible.

'What?' I said.

He looked up. 'What? Oh yes! Well . . . y'know. Bloody difficult. Yuh, yuh.'

There was a long uncomfortable silence. Then Harry reared up from his chair, like a nervous hippo. 'Drunk as fuck,' he said, almost shouting. 'Got to get to bed. Cheer the fuck up, Muller.'

With that, he went off to the guest suite.

I sat for a long while, then, staring up at the starry sky, making myself feel dizzy. After half an hour or so, Penny appeared at the sliding doors, bearing a portable phone. 'Willy, it's your sister calling from London.'

I took the phone. 'Monika?' There were muffled noises of distress on the other end of the line. 'Monika, are you there?'

'Willy,' Monika said, at last. '*Mutti* is dead.'

12

28 *February* 1979

I slept with a married man last night. I met him at the
wine bar down the road from work. He was there on his
own. Sandra from work got talking to him first, but he
was giving me the eye and when she went off to buy fags,
he turned to me and said, quietly, 'Do you want to get
out of here?' Just that, no introduction. Oh God, it was
so sexy – I practically peed myself. I said I couldn't
because of Sandra, so when she came back he asked her
to come along too. It was really freezing out but he made
us walk for ages. He is quite a bit older (thirty-five???)
and no oil painting, but for some reason I was into it. I
think I like them older and a bit ugly. I get fearful and
inhibited in the presence of someone too good-looking.
Good to be the golden young princess surrendering to a
pock-marked old tyrant. Sandra got annoyed at being the
gooseberry after a bit and got a taxi home. We carried on
walking. Smoked a joint. We talked about everything –
he's called Michael, he works in marketing and he lives
in Chiswick with his wife and two kids. I said didn't his
wife mind him wandering around late at night with
strange girls? And he looked at me funnily and said it
wasn't like that and I had to learn about marriage. He
was very ironic and cool. When I told him I wanted to
train in aromatherapy, he laughed and said didn't I have
anything better to do with my time? Finally, when I was
about to pass out, we got a cab and went to Soho – to
some drinking club – dirty and sad with a lot of very

*pissed old guys. We sat in the back and he ordered vodka
gimlets for us – which he said is the only cocktail worth
drinking. By this point, I was knackered and must have
looked like shit. But then he asked me where I lived and
could we go there? I truly didn't want to sleep with him
because I was so tired and feeling so ugly and worn out
and I couldn't really imagine him at the squat. I smiled in
this very calm way and said, 'Oh Michael, let's not. It
wouldn't be wise.' He just looked at me and laughed. At
first I was pissed off but then I started laughing too. This
terrible passivity came over me and I thought, well it's
going to happen so why fight it? We got a taxi here. I
told him he had to be quiet because of the other people
in the house, but he didn't take any notice. Why do you
live in such a shitty place? he said when we got inside. Is
this your experiment in seeing how the other half live? I
hadn't taken the key out of the front door and he had his
hands on my breasts. He pulled my shirt over my head
and then he undid my bra. I kept thinking Marcus or
Lydia was going to walk out and find us plus I felt
ridiculous standing there in the hallway with no top on
but he refused to stop. He undressed me completely –
unzipped my jeans, pulled them down around my ankles.
He laughed and said 'Good girl' when he saw I had no
knickers on. Then he knelt down, took my shoes and
socks off and – to my horror – kissed each of my toes.
He licked me like a cat from my ankles all the way up
the inside of my thighs. I'm leaning against the front
door, unbelievably embarrassed and turned on. I'm
thinking JESUS CHRIST. He's still completely dressed
which is freaking me out but he won't let me undo
anything. He asks me where the bedroom is and I point
and he says, Let's go and then I have to walk in front of
him upstairs into the bedroom with him staring at my
arse, and just as I'm thinking Thank God the lights are*

*off, he starts flicking them on. In the corridor, and then
in the bedroom. He looks around and I think he is going
to say something mean about it but he doesn't – his eyes
are half closed and he's just looking and looking at me,
drinking me in and it's like he's in the sex zone or
something. I tried again to undress him but he wouldn't
let me. He pushed me on the bed and then he undressed
himself while I watched. He was very very beautiful, like
a wrestling angel. A small, tough, brown body, with
dark, soft hair on the chest. He wasn't wearing
underpants either. His penis was very erect and the most
vivid fuchsia. Then he pushed my legs apart and licked
me. He did this for a long time and kept looking up at
me. At first I was sick with self-consciousness, but the
way he did it, after a while I didn't care. Then he started
fucking me. I'm getting wet just thinking about it. I knew
I wasn't going to come so I faked. When he was done, he
held me tight and kissed me all over my face. We drifted
off for a bit – just the most gorgeous, warm soft snooze
and then a little later, I woke to find him licking me all
over again – like I was some incredibly delicious
chocolate. He left at about 4 in the morning – God
knows what he told his wife – and I drifted off into a
lovely sleep. This morning, I woke with a terrible
hangover – head clanging like the alarm at a railway
crossing, the room all thick with the smell of fucking. I
should feel terrible about it but don't – just exhilarated
and wanting to see him again. I think he will call. He
was very cool and collected when he left but in that way
that men are when they are ashamed to reveal
enthusiasm.*

My earliest memories of my mother are of her crying –
strange, high-pitched, precisely articulated sobs that I
would hear, late at night, as I lay in bed in my grandparents'

house in Hamburg. This was shortly after my father died, and we had been forced to return to Germany from Spain. My mother came from a wealthy, gentile family – her father was the heir to a watch-making fortune and her mother's father had been the mayor of Hamburg. She had been warned against marrying Hermann. 'Life with this man,' my grandfather had told her, 'can only bring you unhappiness.' But she had gone ahead anyway and now she had returned to the family seat in shame. My grandparents felt warmly vindicated by my father's premature death and neither of them could set eyes upon my mother without wagging their heads in a sort of gleeful remorse.

To escape them, she spent most of her time locked in her childhood bedroom, reading romantic novels and eating boxes and boxes of marzipan. Sometimes, she would emerge from her room and come down to the nursery, where my sister and I played under the supervision of a rather terrifying Bavarian nanny. Tear-stained and newly plump from all the marzipan, my mother would sit and watch us playing before suddenly swooping down on us to clutch us in tight, damp embraces.

She was not mourning so much as sulking. She never expressed any animus towards the Nazis who had forced her husband to flee the country – she accepted their authority as complacently and unquestioningly as she did that of her parents. All her rage was reserved for her husband – this ludicrous man who had tainted her with his Jewishness and his silly politics and then dropped dead at the most inconvenient moment. Growing up, my sister and I received a puzzlingly contradictory set of impressions of our late father. He had been staggeringly mean and selfish, we gathered, but also comically inept. As time went on, we learned to resent this bumbling Satan almost as much as our mother did. He'd left us with *her*, hadn't he?

Before marrying, my mother had been a dancer of some

repute, and when we first returned to Hamburg there was some talk of her teaching dance or even starting up a little dance school. But her enthusiasm for this idea soon waned, and, since her parents seemed prepared to support us all indefinitely, there was no immediate incentive to find work. Left to her own devices, she would probably have slipped into a life of moody inertia. But early in May of 1937 she was summoned to an interview with the Gestapo. Their motivation in arranging this meeting was unclear – perhaps even to themselves. The two officers who received her in a grandiose office on *Gastlerstrasse* claimed to be interested in extracting information from her about her late husband's political affiliations, but the actual questions they asked suggested a more purely ideological exercise. 'How did it feel to have sexual relations with a Jew-boy?' they asked my mother. 'Do you love your Jew children?' Towards the end of the meeting, which lasted about an hour, one of them observed that, as a mother of a Jew's children, she 'was as good as Jewish herself'. Soon afterwards, her parents arranged for us to go 'on holiday' to England, where my mother took a job teaching movement therapy at a mental asylum in Totnes.

Everyone has a story that they cling to as their Ur-story – the narrative that in some way sums up or defines their life. My mother's was her escape from Germany. My sister and I heard the tale of this journey over and over as we were growing up. On 7 June 1937 we boarded a train at Hamburg station. The journey was without event until we reached the French border. Then a Nazi officer came round to inspect everyone's papers. He hovered for a long time over my mother's travel documents and asked several suspicious questions about her plans. 'We are going to England for a short holiday,' she told him. At which point, I apparently looked up and protested in a loud voice, 'But Mummy, we aren't really going for a holiday. We are going to live in

England. We're going away from the men who don't like Daddy!'

All movement and noise in the carriage stopped dead, my mother said. She remembered looking at the woman sitting opposite her – a pointy-nosed *hausfrau* carrying an extremely expensive leather handbag – and thinking, *It's all over.*

But, miraculously, it wasn't. Perhaps the officer hadn't heard what I said. Perhaps he dismissed it as childish fantasy. Or perhaps he took pity on my mother. In any case, he went away and we were allowed to go on. For many years afterwards, it was my mother's habit, whenever she was displeased with her children, to shout at us, 'I should have told that officer the truth and let him take you to the camps!' (Later on, when more was known, she amended the curse to '. . . and let him take you to the ovens!', but by that time I had learned how to drive her crazy by turning away, pretending to hide a smirk.)

Penny insisted on coming to London with me, of course. She brought about twenty items of luggage and a carry-on gunny sack, bulging with cans of mineral water to spray on her face, breath mints, health-food snacks, eye-shades and magazines. Thankfully, she spent most of the flight ensconced in some vagina novel called *Bringing It On Home*, leaving me to think gloomy thoughts about my mother in peace.

Walking through the arrivals terminal at Heathrow, I was embarrassed by my appearance, which is all wrong for England – too wealthy-looking, too smooth and sunned. Penny is also wildly out of place, with her cantilevered tits and mincing gait. I had forgotten the way that English women stomp about like navvies. 'Take your sunglasses off,' I ordered, but she refused. On the way out to the taxi stand I saw a man sitting in the terminal's 'village' of restaurants, eating baked beans and a long, thin, undercooked sausage. *Ah*, I thought, *England*.

In the taxi on the way into the city, Penny affected great, sighing pleasure at the sight of the terraced houses next to the motorway. She has visited England a couple of times before with former boyfriends and hasn't liked it much (bad food and nothing to watch on TV but news shows and documentaries about sparrows), but she has a dim notion that it is classy to appreciate underdeveloped places, so she never admits to her distaste. The hotel I booked, on Monika's recommendation, is a small, pretentious town-house in Holland Park – voile-swagged, over-heated, claustrophobic. When we got to our room, Penny immediately repaired to the bathroom. I flipped my shoes off, remoted the TV on and climbed aboard the lace-choked four-poster. Behind the bathroom door, as I flicked sceptically through the room-service menu, I could hear the frantic spraying and brushing noises of Penny attempting to mend the ravages of her plane journey. There is something very disheartening about the way middle-aged females dash about, trying to shore up the crumbling parapets of their feminine charm. Discarding the menu (a disaster), I picked up the phone and rang my sister. She answered the phone with her usual gloomy affirmative. 'Yes?'

'Hello, Monika. It's Willy.'

'Hello, darling. Are you in London?'

'Yes. I just got in. How are you?'

'Oh, you know. The arrangements have been completely exhausting.'

'I can imagine. Poor you. What time does it begin tomorrow?'

'The service is at 10. At Golders Green Cemetery. It's a cremation, by the way. She specified. Afterwards, there's a reception at my flat.'

'Okay, good. Will Sophie be coming?'

'Well, no, actually. She said she didn't want to.'

'Ah.'

'Is your friend with you?'

'Yes, she's here.'

There was a silence.

'Oh, another thing. Don't send or bring flowers. She specified that, too. Donations to your charity of choice.'

'Ah, cheery to the last.'

Monika laughed miserably.

Afterwards, I called Puerto Vallarta to check on Harry. The answerphone picked up, but instead of Sissy Yerxa's message, there was Harry, speaking in a high-pitched Mexican accent. 'Helloooo! I am Willy's new girlfriend. I'm fifteen but very old for my age, and I like Madonna, going to the mall and seeing any movie with Tom Cruise in it. Leave a message if you like and I'll make sure Willy gets back to you. Here come's the beep . . .'

I paused, wondering who might have called and heard this message. 'Harry,' I said. 'If you're there, pick up.'

Silence.

'Okay, Harry, do me a favour. Change the message, will you? I'm not amused.'

13

20 *August 1979*

Michael is very mean to me – he'll see some stain on my jumper, or spot on my face, and point at it like a headmaster admonishing a student for an inkblot. 'What's that?' he says. Lydia says he's a sadist, a narcissist. He's not the sort of boyfriend your friends like. He's the sort everyone thinks is a bad lot. When he puts his mouth to my ear, he seems to drool great volumes of spittle into my ear drum. He wears crisp, £200 white shirts made in France that he leaves crumpled on my scummy carpet. Should I make more effort? No – it's the squalor he likes. Squalor to set off him so immaculate. He's a dandy. A mean dandy. His ties make subtle reference to the flecks of colour in his jacket. Anything that smacks of connoisseurship, of complicated or educated taste – that's what appeals to Michael. Says I undervalue these things because I come from privilege. Wrong, wrong, but this is a fantasy that he seems to like – me being some hoity toity little bitch he is taking down a peg or two. Only thing I cannot abide is the way his voice turns all preachy and serious when he speaks about his wife or his kids. You are a good laugh, the voice says, but please don't imagine you can share with me the truly important things in life. Sometimes he will refer to my being young and not having kids in this horribly smug way, as if parenthood were the essential piece of experience required to speak with him on equal terms. How bloody convenient. Our sex is the best thing I've ever done in my life. Like every split second of sensory happiness I've ever had – sun on my back, cold air in my lungs – all rolled into one and lasting for hours and hours. The light in the room changes; it's always dusk. Our skin goes together. Oh, you beautiful girl, he says. And I think, What? Who? Our bodies fit. No rubberiness. He's never exactly romantic, but when he's in bed he's very kind. I just feel so loved. He says, 'Give it to me, give it to me. Give it up,' in this sex-zone murmur. Or just, 'I'm fucking you.' I'm stunned that someone should find that statement of fact a source of excitement. Sometimes when he's getting dressed – never when he's in bed with me – he talks about 'pussy' – which I dont like at all, so twee and aggressive at the same time. Call it cunt, I tell him, but he doesn't listen. Would never do anything I'd instructed is the thing. When he gets up to go, I lie there all limp and pink-cheeked watching him revert to bastardness. Sometimes I will give in and say do you have to go now? and he will shout at me. Another lie we conspire in – that he is 'selfish' – that I would like him to be more 'considerate'. But something in me enjoys his badness. Being hard done by is an underrated pleasure. Even when he says nasty things to me I'm afraid I rather love it. It's odd, but being treated badly is a sort of liberation – a moral holiday. I really think I'm in love.

Penny insisted on attending my mother's funeral in the most ostentatious mourning outfit – black lace everything, including a veil, and special, outsized funeral sunglasses. Monika, who was also wearing sunglasses – black and gold ones to match her black and gold coat – seemed to take against Penny on sight. She had brought her mo friend, Geoffrey, and the two of them kept staring at Penny's veil and breaking into titters. With the exception of my two daughters – who are exempted by virtue of blood-tie –

Monika has never liked women much. 'Why would I?' she replied tartly when I pointed this out to her, once. 'They want the same things I do.'

There were ten or twelve of my mother's friends in the chapel – most of them middle-aged beardies in sandals who had studied with her after she left the Totnes loony bin. (Late in life, my mother became something of a guru in the movement-therapy world.) As I entered the chapel, I could feel them all eyeing me with shy curiosity. Here was the saintly Ursula's evil offspring!

I sat with Monika, Geoffrey and Penny in the front pew, studying the curls of hospital green paint peeling away from the walls and the three adolescent undertakers lolling about, picking at their carbuncles. It would have given my mother satisfaction, I think, to have known in what lugubriously English circumstances she would receive her final send-off. She devoted the better part of her life to hating England – its ugliness, its rudeness, its failure to recognize her social and spiritual superiority. She could have returned to Germany after the war, but, by then, hating England had become a sort of drug. It suited her better to remain here, pretending that she was living in enforced exile and luxuriating in her foreigner's contempt: 'Oh, these rotten little cockneys with their tea-cakes!'

After about ten minutes of hanging around, a loud whirring announced the arrival of my mother's coffin, rising up out of the floor like an old-fashioned cinema organ. The chapel hydraulics seemed rather dodgy and the coffin's juddering ascent was painfully slow and noisy. Presently I felt the vibrations of Monika and Geoffrey shaking with silent giggles. Once the coffin had come to a halt, the vicar, or whoever he was, stood up and walked to the lectern. 'Welcome,' he said. 'Welcome, friends and relations of Ursula Muller – and a special welcome to her two children, who knew her best as "*Mutti*".'

I could feel Monika nudging me furiously at this point, but I refused to look at her. I wasn't feeling particularly reverent about my mother's deadness, or about the vicar, but I do despise that ghastly, 'You've got to laugh, haven't you?' approach to religious occasions. As a young man, I often goaded my believing friends with crudely logical questions about God. But as the years have passed, I have found myself hankering more and more for a little cosy voodoo in my life. Increasingly, I regard my atheism as a regrettable limitation. It seems to me that my lack of faith is not, as I once thought, a triumph of the rational mind, but rather, a failure of the imagination – an inability to tolerate mystery: a species, in fact, of neurosis. There is no chance of my being converted, of course – it is far too late for that. But I wish it wasn't.

When the vicar was done talking, the undertakers loped forward to shift the coffin on to a little conveyor belt. As the belt jolted into action and my mother began her last wobbly journey through the chapel's curtained coffin-hatch, Geoffrey leaped up and pressed a button on a large tape player that Monika had brought with her. The music Monika had chosen was Elisabeth Schwarzkopf singing an aria from the *St Matthew Passion*. (I have to assume this was Geoffrey's influence, since I've never known Monika to listen to anything other than show-tunes.) Penny and a few of the hippies cried. Monika and I stared at the floor.

Since there was no burial – my mother's remains are to be stored next to the chapel in a sort of stone filing cabinet – there was nothing for the mourners to do after the service but go straight to the wake at Monika's flat. Somehow, Penny and I ended up with two of the elderly hippies in a taxi. Penny wittered away at them – leaving them mute and glazed-eyed at her brazen silliness, while I, taking advantage of my status as premier mourner, gazed silently out of the window.

*

When Oona died, the funeral was held at a Quaker meeting hall in Hampstead. Margaret, who arranged the whole thing, invited people to stand up and share their memories of Oona – not a good idea. In addition to being criminally dull, several of those who spoke seemed to have only the most tenuous claims to intimacy with the deceased. Death and dying, I have often noticed, bring out a competitive spirit in people. Who shall emerge as the dearest friend, the closest confidante, of the corpse? One cheeky little fuck, claiming to be a former lover of Oona's, rattled on in excruciating detail about their relationship's 'erotic dimension'.

Sophie and Sadie read poems – Margaret's idea also, I suppose, although I never actually enquired. There was something exploitative about enlisting the girls in that way, I thought. It had the same obscene cuteness as small children dressed in miniature versions of adult clothes. I can't remember what Sophie's poem was, but Sadie, I know, read 'Another Weeping Woman' by Wallace Stevens. She recited tearlessly – almost gaily. Naturally, her performance brought the house down.

Was my mother there? No – that's right, she had called me that morning, as I was setting off, to tell me she wasn't coming. *What is it you have done, Willy? There are reporters outside my door. Men with cameras and lights. What is it you have done?* The reporters were outside the Quaker hall, too, when I got there – mostly spotty little boys from the tabs, but also a few guys from the broadsheets and a couple of TV crews. I knew some of them. There was one man from London Weekend Television who I had been out drinking with on several occasions. He wore the same expression as the rest of them – a sort of swivel-eyed sheepishness overlaid with defiance. *Fair cop*, the expression said. *You know the game, Willy. You'd have done the same thing in our shoes.*

Scumbags.

I never vultured a *funeral*.

In the papers the next day, anonymous 'friends of the family' attested that I had been scandalously dry-eyed throughout the proceedings: HUBBY BILL DIDN'T SHED A TEAR.

It was a pretty grim scene at Monika's flat – 3-litre boxes of sweet white wine and tough canapés that the hippies chewed at enthusiastically with their rabbity teeth. I wandered around, nodding at people, avoiding conversations. Monika is, it seems, as slovenly as ever. In her bathroom there was one dried out sliver of soap, veined with dirt, and an overflowing laundry basket giving off a vaguely genital tang. Her bedroom floor was littered with discarded garments, and on the (unmade) bed a tray of some putrid, half-eaten snack sat fizzing with bacteria. I wound up in Mort's old den (where a full cat-litter tray had been plonked in the fireplace) and was just starting to make my way through Mort's vast collection of *Playboy*s when Monika came in and found me.

'Did we have miserable childhoods, Monika?' I asked her.

She smiled and rubbed her eyes. 'I should say so.' She doesn't look bad for an old lady, Monika. Good bones. Ten years ago, she could still bring the visiting room at the Scrubs to a standstill. She used to teeter across the room with her rabbit-fur coat perched on her shoulders like a mantel, while the inmates bored holes in her with their eyes. 'Tell me when they start to drool,' she would say slyly, as she sat down.

'But it doesn't explain why I am a shit, does it?' I asked her now.

'What?'

'I mean, you've always been good, and, if anything, *Mutti* hated you more than me. Why am I such a shit?'

'Darling, I'm not so good and you're not a shit. You're just . . . troubled.' I imagined Monika describing me this way to her friends. 'Oh, my *troubled* brother, Willy . . .'

'Really?' I said. 'Is that really how you think of me?'

'Not in a bad way, darling . . .'

I shook my head. I didn't want any more of this conversation.

'So . . . did *Mutti* leave us anything?'

Monika grunted derisively. 'Oh sure. I get her collection of electric blankets and you get her Yogomagic.'

'Really? Was there no money?'

'About five thousand pounds in the bank which she left for Sophie and Sadie . . .'

'How is Sophie?' I asked. 'How is her little boy?'

Monika exhaled heavily. 'Oh, Sophie's all right. Jack's all right. He's almost seven, you know. The boyfriend's a bit . . . They've got a council flat near Holborn. Willy, why don't you go and see her, while you're here?'

'God, no.'

'Why?'

'Just, no.'

'Don't be silly.'

'Don't you be silly. Sophie hates me.'

'No she doesn't. She has a lot of anger towards you . . .'

'Okay, she has a lot of anger. Why would I want to get yelled at?'

'First, no one's going to yell at you – well, she might. But that's how things get sorted out. Go on.'

'Ach . . . no, I don't think so. She wouldn't want to see me.'

Monika picked up the phone and waggled the receiver at me. 'Why don't you call her and find out?'

I jerked away from the proffered phone. 'Nah.'

'*Go* on.'

'What would I say?'

'Just say "Hello, how are you? Would you like to meet up some time while I'm here in London?" Say whatever you want.'

I took the receiver from her outstretched hand. It smelled of her powdery perfume and it was speckled with flecks of her make-up. I adjusted my grip so that I held the phone between my thumb and forefinger, a couple of inches from my face. Monika punched out the number.

'Is it ringing?' she whispered.

'I think so,' I said, straining to hear.

'Hello?' someone said very faintly. It was Sophie's voice.

'Hello. Is that Sophie?'

'Yeah. Who's this?'

'Sophie, it's your dad.' Out of the corner of my eye I could see Monika, who was sitting on the arm of my chair now, making furious thumbs-up signals.

'Hello,' Sophie said. 'You sound very distant.'

'I'm here in London.'

'Yeah, I heard.' She spoke with a working-class drawl. When did that happen? What is that about?

'I'm over at Auntie Monika's right now – we're just back from your grandmother's funeral.'

'I can't hear you.'

Reluctantly, I brought the soiled receiver a fraction closer to my lip. 'I said, we've just got back from your grandmother's funeral.'

'Oh yeah?'

'Yeah.' Silence. 'I was just saying to Monika that I would like to see you before I go back.'

A long pause.

'Hello?' I said.

'Yeah?'

'Sorry, I thought I'd lost you for a second . . . So, yes, would it be okay if I came to see you?'

There was more pause.

'Sophie?'

'I don't mind,' she said abruptly.

I laughed awkwardly. 'Well, all right then. What about tomorrow?'

'Whatever.'

'When would be a good time?'

'Whatever.'

'Would around two be good?'

'All right.'

'Right. Okay. Are you sure this is okay for you?'

'Yeah, it's okay.'

'Well now, where do you ... oh, I suppose Auntie Monika can give me your address.'

'Yeah.'

'Okay. Good. I'll see you tomorrow then.'

'Yeah, all right.'

'See you then.'

'Seeya.'

I put down the phone.

'Good for you!' Monika said. 'You'll be glad you did this.' She got up from her chair. 'I should really go back out there and see that everyone's all right.'

'Yes,' I said. 'I'll join you in a second.'

Monika opened the door to the living room, letting in a momentary drone of wine-glass clinking and chatter. I repaired to the guest bathroom, where I tore off several sheets of lavatory paper, dampened them under the hot tap and applied them anxiously to my mouth and the ear where the phone had touched.

14

*I went away with Michael this weekend. He had a
conference in Brighton and booked a little hotel away
from all his colleagues so I could go too. I think I
behaved pretty unattractively. I am late, which always
makes me feel miserable and bloated. It was a sad time
and I got quite down, being left on my own all day and
not being able to go out with him in the evenings. (He
was so paranoid, he made me sit in the bathroom when
room service came.) He was horrible a lot of the time –
shouting at me to stop being so fucking miserable. His
wife called twice. He was quite bad-tempered with her
too, which cheered me up. One time, she put his
daughter on the phone and I heard him call her
'Babaloo', which was weird because that's what he calls
me. Maybe that's quite sweet in a way. One night he
started talking about how beautiful women aren't good
at sex. 'Their beauty makes them passive,' he says. 'It's
the years of adulation, you know.' I kept nodding and
nodding until I thought my head was going to fall off
and roll across the floor. I thought, He doesn't think I'm
beautiful. That's why he can say this to me because it's
so obvious – it so goes without saying – that I am not.
He kept on and on. 'They expect everything to be done
to them which is a bore and actually rather exhausting in
the long run.' On reflection, I think he knew exactly
what he was doing. He just wanted to fuck with my
head. On the train back to London, he saw a load of*

people on the platform who he knew in marketing, and it was total aggro. He made me sit on a seat away from him to be safe. Every time I looked round he was reading the paper and didn't even acknowledge me. Then, when we were getting off the train, a man came up and started talking to him, so we didn't even get to say goodbye.

This afternoon, I set off in a cab to see Sophie. (Penny had wanted to accompany me, but after some argument and the handing over of substantial sums of cash, she settled for a shopping trip to Knightsbridge instead.) The journey took three quarters of an hour – giving me ample opportunity to fret and dither about the wisdom of this little adventure. The memory of Sophie's proletarianized accent, together with the grimey-sounding Holborn address to which I was heading, accounted for a fair amount of my anxiety. I am particularly unfond of the British working class and saddened at the notion of my daughter electing, if not to join their ranks, then to mimic their manners and parlance. That both my children should have ended up scorning the privileges of their own class is mystifying to me. I am not an idiot – I know that little rich girls want their bit of rough. But it's not as if Sadie and Sophie ran away with the raggle-taggle gypsies-o. They got themselves council flats and illegitimate babies and the grey drear of lumpen Englishness. This is not snobbery on my part – at least not in the way that is normally meant by that term. I have a fairly vehement dislike of all British social classes. Nor is it ignorance: my boyhood spent among the lower orders of Totnes gives me some claim to authority on this matter. On the basis of my interactions with the dwarfish plebs of Devonshire, I can vouch with confidence that there is no socio-economic group in the world quite as viciously ignorant and cruel as the British working class.

Before leaving my hotel room, I had taken the precaution

of dividing the cash in my wallet into two wodges. The thin one I kept in the wallet; the thick one – a sum of approximately three hundred pounds – I stashed in my left sock. This was a nancy sort of thing to do. I was aware that it was nancy even as I was doing it. But it afforded me some comfort, I can tell you, when my taxi drew up on a urinous alleyway just off Chancery Lane and I was forced to disembark.

The 'estate' in which Sophie lives is comprised of four red-brick Victorian blocks, each one named after a great British novelist. The blocks are arranged around a laundry-festooned courtyard in which, when I arrived, twenty or so small children were racing about, shouting at each other in hoarse, angry voices. Since Sophie resides on the penulti-mate floor of the Defoe building and the generosity of the council does not run to providing elevators, I was forced to climb four flights of predictably unpleasant stairs in order to reach her. At the top I paused for a moment to catch my breath. As I stood, panting heavily, feeling the rasp of cash on my left ankle, I saw a tall young woman emerge from her flat at the end of the balcony. She had a pale face and long dark hair that flopped forward as she leaned over the iron railings. 'Jack!' she shouted. 'I've told you three fucking times. Get up here now!' I recognized the gargled vowels from the phone call the day before. She turned now and disappeared back into the flat. I walked slowly along the balcony until I reached the door she had just slammed. I hesitated for a moment, and then I flapped the letterbox. The door swung open almost immediately. A tall, frighteningly skinny man stood swaying slightly on the threshold. He had shoulder-length dirty hair, swept back in a pony-tail, and small, deeply set eyes that seemed to be all pupil. His skin was a terrible yellow – the colour of old pillows. In the middle of his forehead, there was a giant purple scab.

'Hello,' he said, bleakly.

I smiled, or I think I did. 'Hello,' I said. 'I'm looking for Sophie.'

The man turned around. 'Sophie!' he yelled. Somewhere in the murky recess of the flat a door opened and Sophie appeared. There was a strange, satirical half-smile on her lips as she came forward. She was almost beautiful, I saw.

'All right, Dad?' she said.

The accent, I realized now, was a very poor imitation. It was too much and not enough; the intonation was wrong. Poor Sophie. She sounded like Audrey Hepburn in *My Fair Lady*.

'Hello!' I said. My voice had a quaver in it.

Sophie gestured at the tall man. 'This is Nial.'

'Hello!' I said again. *Enough with the Hellos already.* I stepped forward to embrace Sophie, or to shake Nial's hand – I didn't know which. But both of them had already turned and were leading the way into a small, chaotic living room, littered with toys and the detritus of a McDonald's repast.

'Siddown,' Sophie said, pointing to a two-seater sofa.

I sat. To my dismay, Nial sat next to me, his thighs almost touching mine. Sophie remained standing.

'D'ya wanna cupatea then?' she asked.

I nodded. 'That would be lovely.' Sophie went out to the kitchen. I remained sitting, wondering how to remedy the horrifying fact of Nial's proximity. Tiny beadlets of perspiration were pricking up across my back. From out of the corner of my eye, I could see deposits of greenish scum gathered at the corners of Nial's mouth.

'Well, this is a cosy little place,' I said.

Nial appeared not to hear this. At any rate, he did not respond. Then he suddenly shouted something. It was incomprehensible at first, but after a few moments' reflection I gathered that he was requesting a sandwich from Sophie.

'It's good to meet you at last,' I said. (This is the sort of thing that people mean when they talk about 'soldiering on'.) 'I've heard a lot about you from Sophie's Aunt Monika.'

Nial giggled. It was a terrible, high-pitched giggle. I struggled not to be terrified. Then he began to sing.

'Morning has broken, like the first morning; blackbird has spoken, like the first bird . . .'

A tiny white globule of spittle contracted and expanded between his big grey lips. I stayed very still. *My daughter kisses those lips*, I thought.

'Kettle's on,' Sophie said, coming in with a white-bread sandwich on a plate. She handed it to Nial. 'It's cheese and mayonnaise,' she announced. Nial took the plate and began to gobble up the sandwich noisily.

Sophie looked at me. She was smiling her hard half-smile again.

'Don't worry. He's having a turn.'

'Ah,' I nodded.

'D'ya see Jack when you was coming up?' Sophie asked.

'Jack? Well, yes, I probably did – but I didn't know which one was him.'

'He's the fat one with a filthy fackin gob on im,' Nial said, his mouth full of sandwich.

Sophie laughed. I was trying to think of something to say when the kettle began to whistle in the kitchen. 'I won't be a sec,' Sophie said, getting up. She came back carrying two mugs of tea. 'D'ya take sugar?' she asked, kneeling down in front of the two of us.

'No thanks.'

'Here you go then.'

She handed me one of the mugs. The tea was strong – brick-coloured – and the mug was dirty. I put it down on the floor.

'So, have you been well?' I asked. 'You look well. I'd forgotten how pretty you are.'

134

Sophie laughed again – a dismissive, hollow-sounding hoot. 'Go away!' she said, flapping her hands at me.

Nial had begun to rock back and forth now. 'You think so?' he was saying, over and over, experimenting with different emphases. 'You *think* so? You think *so*? *You* think so?' He plucked roughly at his scab. Blood immediately began trickling down his yellow forehead. 'Don't pick yer scab, Nial!' Sophie shouted. 'Look, see, now yer bleeding. Go into the toilet and get yerself some loo roll. Go on.'

I could feel myself beginning to tremble uncontrollably. Nial got up from the sofa and strode across the living room, bent over at an angle of 45 degrees, like Groucho Marx. I looked at my daughter. There was some part of her that seemed to be hovering over this scene, enjoying its impressive awfulness.

We sat for a moment in silence, listening to Nial crash about in the bathroom and then the kitchen.

'Is everything all right?' I asked. But before Sophie could reply, there was a scream from the hallway, and the next moment Nial came running in with a piece of lavatory paper blotting his bloody forehead and an ice-tray in his left hand. 'Sophe!' he yelled. 'Help me, Sophe!' His fingers had become stuck to the fur of frost on the tray's outer rim. 'I was trying to make a vodka and tonic, wasn't I?' he explained plaintively.

Sophie got up, fetched a tea towel and hastily prised the tray out of Nial's hand. Nial howled. A yellowish smear of flesh from his index finger was left on the side of the tray. 'It hurts!' Nial bellowed. I could feel pre-nausea saliva flooding into my mouth. Sophie pushed Nial out of the living room. 'Go and get a plaster, wally,' she instructed. She turned back to me, shaking her head and tittering slightly. 'I've got to take Jack to the doctor's in a bit. D'ya wanna wait here, or come with?'

As she and I walked down through the estate, Sophie

exchanged greetings with a number of female neighbours – sometimes shouting out to acquaintances on balconies across the courtyard in a piercing, prole yodel.

'All right, Meechelle?'

'All right, Sophe?'

'How's it going?'

'Not too bad. Seeya then.'

'Yeah. Seeya.'

Down in the courtyard, Sophie called to one of the playing children. 'Jack, come ere! Nah!' A solidly corpulent boy with a shaven head emerged from the herd and walked towards us. He wore a Tottenham Hotspur soccer kit. 'Jack, this is your granddad,' Sophie said. 'Say hello.' The little boy stared up at me. 'Ullo!' he bellowed, obligingly. I attempted to arrange my features in an appropriate grand-fatherly set. 'C'mon, Jack,' Sophie said. 'Get your coat – we gotta go and see Doctor Rolfe.' Jack ran off obediently to pick up a lurid orange anorak from where he had left it hanging on a bollard.

'What's he seeing the doctor for?' I asked.

'It's a psychiatrist. He goes once a week, for ferapy.'

'Why's that?'

'He's hyperactive, isn't he,' Sophie replied. 'Drives me mad.'

Jack came running back now, and together the three of us walked through the archway of the estate, out on to the roaring street. Sophie pointed to a parked pale blue van. 'That's Nial's,' she said. On its battered side was painted the legend

NIAL THE CHIPPIE
High standards and Competative prices
Call 910 3590

'Is Nial, um, working at the moment?' I asked.

'Oh yeah,' Sophie said. 'He's building shelves for some

Paki butchers in the east end.' There was something like wifely pride in her voice. 'He's thinking about chucking it in, though,' she added, 'cos he's a vegetarian and it's against his principles, yeah?'

We walked towards Clerkenwell, passing large Victorian warehouses and grey sixties office buildings and small sparsely stocked supermarkets, with handwritten signs in their windows advertising cut prices. It was one of those English winter days when the sun juts in and out of vast, racing cloudbanks and the air is cold and pale and bright at the same time. Jack ran ahead, picking up litter from the street, poking with experimental meanness at dogs tied to lampposts and chattering wildly to himself.

I was just a little older than him when I first came to England. My mother used to work late at the loony bin and Monika had no interest in babysitting me, so after school I was free to wander the outskirts of town, making lonely mischief. I used to tie one end of a cotton thread around a lamppost and the other around some railings and lie in wait for people to come and trip over it. I would make vats of ersatz vomit out of chopped-up grass, water and red mud and pour it on people's front doorsteps. Sometimes, I stole sweets from the tobacconist near my school. Once, after a successful raid, I was down by the river, throwing stolen sweet wrappers into the water, when the postman came past on his bicycle.

'What do you'm think you're doing?' he shouted at me.

'Nothing,' I replied, mechanically.

The postman got off his bike and wheeled it closer to me. 'I seen you, littering the river,' he said. 'You little bugger.' He stared at me, menacingly. Then he got back on his bike. 'I know you!' he had shouted, as he retreated. 'You'm be a Jerry!'

After a while, Jack came back and trotted alongside us, asking me questions.

'You my granddad?' he asked.

'Yes,' I replied.

'Whass yer name?'

'Willy.'

Jack giggled.

'Shut up,' Sophie told him sharply.

'Where d'ya live then?' Jack asked.

'California. America.'

'You really my granddad?'

'Absolutely.'

'Did yer bring me a present?'

'Shut up, Jack. Spoiled brat,' Sophie said.

I marvelled at how the little boy rebounded from his mother's spitting reprimands.

'You don't sound like a Yank,' Jack said now.

'That's because I'm not,' I said.

'Ow old are you?'

We were on a small side street, approaching a rather impoverished-looking pub called the Goat and Compass.

'I am twenty-one,' I said, with leaden playfulness.

'No you aint!' Jack shouted, delightedly.

Outside the pub, a man and a woman were arguing – the woman standing against the pub-front and the man facing her, steadying himself against the wall with both of his hands.

'I never said vat, ya cunt!' the woman exclaimed as we neared. I prayed silently that the man would not hit her – or at least not until we had safely passed by. 'Oi, Sophie!' the woman cried suddenly, looking over the man's shoulder. *Oh, Christ, please don't let her ask us to intervene*, I thought. But the woman did not want help. 'All right, Sophe?' she cried.

'All right?' Sophie said.

We passed on.

In another five minutes we came to a large hospital

building opposite a park. Sophie stopped at the foot of the hospital steps. 'I'll be back to collect yer in an hour,' she told Jack.

'What are you two going to do now?' Jack asked.

'I don't know,' Sophie snapped. 'Go on, you'll be late.'

'Seeya!' Jack yelled at me. Then he turned and ran up the steps.

'Do you wanna go home or have a walk in the park, then?' Sophie asked.

'A walk would be nice,' I said. I was feeling exhausted, and my temples were throbbing with the early warning signs of a headache, but I would have done anything to avoid returning to that flat and having to confront the monstrous Nial again.

The park was a dreary place, dotted with dog shit and spindly council trees bundled up in wire netting. Even the grass seemed a peculiarly grey shade of green. A terrible wave of sadness passed over me as Sophie and I trudged up one of the asphalt paths. Her affected accent seemed a great barrier between us. I felt that if she broke down for a moment and spoke to me honestly, it would be in her old, upper-middle-class voice. 'Here we go,' she said, plonking herself down on the grass. 'Less siddown.'

I inspected the grass for shit and then took off my jacket and sat down on it. For several minutes we sat in silence, enjoying the pale sun on our faces. I wanted to say something about Sadie but I couldn't think how to introduce the subject. I turned to look at Sophie. She and Sadie both inherited from me a face that looks angry and wretched in repose. Something to do with the set of the lips. For a man, it's not so bad – perhaps even an asset. But it's not a nice thing for a young woman. Even as little girls, they were always being told to cheer up, it might never happen.

'Jack seems a very sweet boy,' I said. 'He has a lot of Oona in him.'

Sophie tucked her hair behind her ears. 'Yeah, people say that,' she said. This surprised me. He didn't really seem like Oona – I had only said it to be nice.

'And . . . so tell me,' I asked, 'does he ever see his real father?'

'Nah.'

'How long has he been seeing this psychiatrist?'

'Six monfs. The school made him go. Cos he's disruptive in class.'

'I must say, you're pretty brisk with him.'

Sophie made a snorting noise and rolled over on to her front. I paused, studying her prone form. Her arse is too flat and wide. She has a good long back, though – like her mother's. When she was a young teenager, I often had sexual thoughts about Sophie. I say sexual, you will note, rather than lustful. They were more inquisitive day-dreams than black-hearted fantasies. I just wondered what her bed manners were going to be like. Was that disgusting of me? Yes, I suppose it was. It's in the nature of truly perverse people to always be supposing or hoping that their perversity is actually standard and universal.

'So whatya been up to then, Dad?' Sophie had turned her head and was staring at me with her pale, sardonic eyes.

'Oh, you know,' I said. 'Well, there's been this heart business for one thing . . .' My headache had begun to blossom now.

'Oh yeah,' Sophie said, pulling up a clump of grass. 'I heard about that. You all right now, are you?'

I admit it, I was hurt. It's hard to say what I had expected – but it was something more than this polite complacency.

'Yes,' I said. 'Not too bad. Can't complain.' I paused. 'Now, this man of yours,' I smiled weakly. 'Is *he* all right?'

Sophie shrugged. 'Yeah, it's just a turn, do you know what I mean? He'll be all right by tomorrow.'

I nodded, trying to look credulous. 'So, with Nial . . . is it, er . . . is it drugs?'

'Yeah,' she said. 'Nial's an addict.'

'Right. I see.' I was embarrassed by her lack of guile. 'Well, that's not good, is it? I must say, he seems in quite a bad way.'

'Addiction's a disease,' she said, rather sharply.

'Yes,' I said. 'Of course. But oughtn't he to be in some sort of treatment?'

Sophie sucked her teeth impatiently. 'No one can elp Nial till Nial wants to elp imself,' she chanted. 'He's gotta reach rock bottom. Do you know what I mean?'

'Hmm, I see. But surely . . .'

Sophie gave one of her sardonic hoots and pulled up another great clump of grass. 'Listen, right, it isn't really any of your business, is it? Do you know what I'm saying?'

I nodded. I knew what she was saying. 'You're quite right, Sophie.' We both looked away from each other.

'Tell me,' I said, brightly, after a while, 'how is Pearl?'

'All right, I think. I don't see her much.'

'Do you and Margaret talk?'

Sophie looked at me with raised eyebrows. 'Oh, yeah. All the time. We exchange recipes.'

I laughed. Sophie watched me with that surprised, proud expression that people wear when they have been amusing without really trying. After a bit, she began to laugh too.

When we stopped, there was an awkward silence. I think she was frantic that I would try to capitalize on the golden moment by saying something meaningful.

'Are you going to see her?' she asked.

'Who, Margaret?'

'Pearl.'

'No, I don't think so. I have to get back to Mexico. I have a lot of work waiting.'

'Oh.'

'Sophie, what I was saying before about Nial . . . I didn't mean to criticize, I was just concerned.'

She made a sceptical, snorting noise.

I began stuttering. 'No, I mean . . . I would . . . I want . . .'

'Listen,' she interrupted. Her eyes narrowed. 'Don't think you can come back here and start telling me how to run my life, right. Because that's a bit cheeky, all right? Let's face it, Dad, what've you ever done for me?'

Ah, here it was.

'Sophie, I'm not trying to tell you anything . . .'

She was scrambling to her feet now. She looked down at me, her face wonderfully calm. 'Oh piss off, Dad,' she said.

When I got back to the hotel, there was a message from Sophie asking me to call her. I flopped on to my bed and dialled the number.

'Dad,' she said. 'I'm sorry.' I could hear tears in her voice. 'That was my fault. It's just, you know . . . difficult to see you after all this time.'

'No, no,' I said. 'It was *my* fault. I don't know how to talk without offending people.'

'Can we try again?' Sophie asked.

I am an idiot. I was touched. 'Of course,' I said.

'Can we see each other tonight?' she asked.

I paused here. I was exhausted. I needed to sleep.

'I'll come to you,' Sophie added quickly. *Sweet girl*, I thought. *I behave like a shit, neglect her and still she wants my love, my approval.*

'Yes, yes, sure,' I said. 'Come on over.'

By the time Sophie got to the hotel, Penny had arrived back from her shopping trip and she absolutely insisted on coming downstairs with me to meet Sophie in the hotel bar. I was too exhausted by that stage to put up much of a protest. We found her sitting at the bar with a rum and coke and a club sandwich. She had changed tee-shirts. Now she was wearing a pale blue, long-sleeved vee-neck, with the word 'bullshit' printed on the right breast. As she shook Penny's hand, the satirical half-smile I had seen earlier returned to her lips.

'Sophie, this is Penny,' I said. 'Penny, this is Sophie.'

'Oh my *God*, you look so much like your Daddy!' Penny gushed, while I ordered drinks. 'I can't believe it!'

Sophie looked at her coldly. 'Why can't you?'

Penny looked to me, for explanation. 'What?'

'Why can't you believe it?' Sophie said. '*I am* his daughter, you know. Who are you?'

I mumbled some protest here, but Penny waved me to be silent. She put on her understanding expression. 'Actually, Sophie,' she said, 'I am a very special friend of your Daddy's.'

Sophie rolled her eyes. 'Oh. So you're fucking him.'

'That's enough,' I said.

Penny got up from her stool. 'I think it would be better if I waited for you upstairs.' She looked at me.

I shrugged. There was no doubt that it would.

She leaned down and patted Sophie's hand. 'Goodbye, Sophie. God bless.'

Left alone, Sophie and I gazed down at our drinks, uneasily.

'That was quite unnecessary,' I said.

Sophie adopted a penitent expression. 'I'm sorry. You're right. I was out of order.'

I was about to dole out some lordly forgiveness, but before I could say anything she added, 'Could you lend me some money?'

I looked at her, taken aback by her gall. She looked straight back.

'What for?' I asked at last.

'For everything . . . for Jack.' Her tone was impatient.

'I have to ask this, Sophie. You don't want money for drugs, do you?'

She glared at me, looking just like Oona. 'If you don't want to give it, just say.'

I paused. She stuffed down more of her club sandwich.

'How much did you want?' There was a strange catch in my voice.

'Whatever you can give, Dad,' she said. Then, hurriedly, 'A couple of hundred?'

I felt a swelling in my chest and the taste of the sea rising at the back of my throat. She was still looking at me steadily – no doubt trying to gauge just how much she was going to be able to sting me for. I felt for my wallet in my jacket pocket, then, remembering the security precautions I had taken earlier in the day, I bent down and reached into my sock.

Sophie's eyebrows rose.

'Don't ask,' I said. I produced the pad of cash and handed it to her. 'There's about three hundred there.'

She put it in her front jeans pocket and took a slug of her drink. For a second, she closed her eyes. 'Ta, Dad.'

Then she got up, put on her denim jacket. I left some money on the bar and walked with her to the door. 'It's all right,' she said at this point, 'you don't have to bother walking me out.' She made a small, pushing-away gesture with her hands. I stopped obediently and stood watching her cross the foyer. At the revolving doors, she turned suddenly and called out to me. Her mouth became jagged and ugly. I couldn't make out what she was saying at first. For a fleeting, stupid moment, I thought that she was shouting something about 'having lunch'. But then, as the door swung behind her, and the concierge turned to stare across the foyer at me, the jumble of sounds came together in my head. 'Murdering cunt,' she had shouted. 'Murdering cunt.'

15

7 November 1979

Morty died. He had an aneurism in the middle of the night. Aunt Monika is in a terrible way. She's not having a funeral, she's getting him cremated and then she's going to scatter his ashes in the Serpentine. Poor thing. They slept in separate rooms and so she only found out he was dead when she took him a cup of tea in the morning. I finally told Michael about being pregnant. It was my birthday last week and he took me out for dinner. Was v. sweet all night. Gave me a silver ring with engraving. It said 'with love', and I cried. Of course, then he had to say, 'I got it big so it'd fit your fat fingers.' I was incredibly antsy all night. Kept being on the verge of tears. When we got home, I told him. He was furious. Immediately asked had I done this on purpose? Was I trying to trap him? I told him not to be such a bastard, I would have an abortion so what the fuck did he care. Then he totally freaked. Didn't I realize how hard this would be for him, how much he hated the idea of destroying a child, blah blah. Okay I said, I'll have it. He kicked my bedside table over and slapped me. Not that hard, but still. Lydia came to the door to ask was I all right. I said yes, I'm fine and he shouted to her to fuck off. I was crying, of course. Then he put his arms around me and said he was sorry.

Yesterday I went into hospital. Told work I was having an ovarian cyst removed, which got a lot of sympathy. I was booked to have it at the women's

hospital on Tottenham Court Road. But the hospital
boiler broke down. NH Fucking S. The waiting room
was filled with pregnant miseries: two thirteen-year-olds
who were friends – I couldn't work that out. Did they get
pregnant at the same time and arrange their abortions for
the same date, on purpose? Also two older women who
kept themselves to themselves. The doctor was this nasty
woman who told me she wanted to put an IUD in me
while I was still under anaesthetic because I obviously
couldn't be trusted to use contraceptives responsibly. I
said I didn't want it because I'd heard it could mess your
insides up and stop you from having a baby later on.
And she just said, oh what nonsense. Silly cow. When I
went for my scan, to check that the baby was big enough
to abort, the woman said, 'Are you sure you don't want
this baby?' You could tell she'd been taught how to
'counsel'. I said I was sure. The machine produced a little
photograph – a fuzzy black and white snapshot with a
little grain of rice marked by two Xs. I said can I keep it?
And she said she wasn't sure – no one had ever asked
before. But she ended up giving it to me. All of the
abortion girls waited together in a small room, wearing
blue surgical smocks that didn't do up properly so we
had to sit clutching ourselves. We watched a morning
show on the television – a woman was on who had
written a book about the classic English tea. She said it
was too bad because the English tea is going into decline
and she demonstrated how to make a perfect cucumber
sandwich. I started to cry, and one of the 13-year-olds,
this very pretty black girl, looked at me sweetly and said,
'Don't be like that. Please. Don't be like that,' which
made me feel ashamed, because bloody hell if she can
cope, being 13, I should too.

After an hour or so, someone came in and said the
boiler had broken down and we all got sent home. Have

to come back next week. Unbelievable. I rang Michael, told him what had happened. He laughed and said this could only happen to you. He said he'd come and pick me up anyway which was v. sweet. I was relieved. I had been certain he would freak out, accuse me of postponing.

'Eeeyeeew, look at your feet,' he said in the taxi. 'They're all bloated.' He was right. They were. I'd taken my shoes off and they looked like uncooked sausages. Something to do with the stress, maybe. Michael said he couldn't stay for long. He sat in Marcus's room and watched TV for a bit – there was some cricket match he wanted to see – and then he came upstairs to my bedroom. 'All right?' he said. He stands weirdly with his hips jutting forward, like a catwalk model. 'I'm cold,' I said. He didn't say anything. 'Are you going to get into bed?' I asked after a while. 'For a bit,' he said. When he got into bed, he lay flat on his back, leaving me to curl around him. 'Take your clothes off,' he said.

'I'm cold.'

'C'mon, you got too much stuff on.'

'It's freezing in here.'

'C'mon.'

'Excuse me?'

'What?'

'I'm not in the mood.'

'Really, you must stop using clichés like that.'

Then he threw back the eiderdown and got out of bed. I thought he was going to go but he stalked into the bathroom and emerged with a pot of the stuff I use to take my eye make-up off.

'What are you doing?' I said.

He got into bed, rolled me over on to my belly and pulled down my pyjama bottoms. 'Let me just try,' he said. 'I'll stop it if you don't like it.' He started running

his finger along the corrugations left by the pyjama
elastic, pushing down my knickers.

I said I know I don't like it already. I was like,
No. Don't. No, don't. I mean it, Michael. But I let
him.

Afterwards, he kissed me quite sweetly on my neck.
How did you like that? I said not a lot, it felt like doing a
shit backwards. He laughed and told me about some
woman he once knew who had multiple orgasms doing it
that way. Bully for her, I said.

I dreamed last night about my own funeral. It was held at
Golders Green, like *Mutti*'s, and the chapel was filled to
capacity with wailing people, none of whom I recognized.
When my coffin came wobbling up out of the floor, it was
open. I was on display. Owing to some strange embalming
process, my corpse had been transformed into a hollow,
plastic vessel, filled with green liquid that gave off a dull
glow. Floating in the liquid were several large artificial
flowers. The mourners were surprised by this, but not
discomfited. They all seemed to be quite pleased. 'What
lovely insides,' one woman said. But then they got in line
to view me up close, and as they filed past their expressions
changed. The chapel became filled with a low murmur of
protest. Finally, the same woman who had praised my
insides shouted, 'This isn't him. We're in the wrong place!'
and everybody began to leave.

When I woke this morning, Penny had already left. She
was spending the day visiting an old girlfriend of hers who
has married an Englishman and now lives in the Cotswolds.
I was meant to be at my mother's flat at nine to help Monika
with sorting through her things, but when the alarm call
came through at seven thirty I was so paralysed by exhaustion
and misery that I simply could not get out of bed. I have
a peculiar horror of post-mortem trawls – the graveyard

smell of dead persons' wardrobes, the medicine cabinets bulging with dusty medicine, the stagey melancholia that the participants must affect in order to disguise their boredom or greed or nosiness. I lay dozing and making sad little bleating noises to myself for several hours, and by the time I mustered enough energy to climb down from the frilly four-poster, it was one o'clock. I tried calling Puerto Vallarta again. Harry still wasn't answering.

'*Hola muchachos!*' the messsage said now. 'I'm far too drunk to answer the phone at the moment . . .'

This was followed by a long crackly pause and the distinct crash of the phone being dropped.

I left another message asking him to call me, then I took a Valium and went down to the lobby to get a cab.

West Hampstead is one of the more impressively lugubrious areas of London, and Rosemont Terrace, where my mother lived, is ground zero of the gloom. Heavy chestnut trees line the street so thickly that, in spring and summer, the branches shut out almost all sunlight. On an autumn day, like today, the pavements are a cake of rotting leaves and sluggy leaf-jam. My mother lived here for twenty years – in a low-ceilinged basement flat that was so damp she had to keep a de-humidifier on night and day to stop her mattress from going green. Apart from an occasional visit from Monika and her movement-therapy students – New Age pilgrims come to worship at her shrine – my mother's only company in her old age was a series of more or less retarded live-in 'helps'. The last time I came to see her here, a lumpy Scandinavian girl greeted me at the door with a torrent of complaints. Mrs Muller woke her up in the middle of the night, she said, demanding foot-baths. Mrs Muller had extreme views on diet and had gone so far as to hit her with a spatula after finding a secret stash of sliced white bread in the larder. Mrs Muller wouldn't let her stay out past ten o'clock at night, even on her days off. If she broke anything – a glass, a soap dish – Mrs Muller insisted on extracting the cost of the item from her meagre wages.

I remember standing in the mouldy-smelling hallway, nodding gravely as the girl tattled on. Her unloveliness depressed me. (Bad enough to be cleaning up my mother for a living, but so much worse to have frazzled hair and be wearing squidgy health-shoes that looked like Cornish pasties.) I drifted off, and as the particulars of her complaint became an indistinct background hum, the fact of her misery seemed to sing out with greater clarity. It was almost a relief after that to be ushered in to the back bedroom where my mother lay, lavishly propped up on seven pillows and smelling faintly of urine. She gaped at me in the half light, soft and wide-eyed like a great, sinister rag-doll. 'Come to *Mutti*,' she gasped. The pendulous wattle connecting her chin and chest flapped as she spoke. I bent over to kiss her. 'What is it, you don't shave any more?' she said, as my cheek touched hers. 'Are you a pimp now, Willy?'

Monika was in the living room when I arrived, rummaging through a chest of drawers. 'Hello, darling,' she said. I could tell from the brightness of her tone and the slightly frantic way she was moving about that she was pissed off with me.

'Sorry I'm late,' I said. 'I overslept.'

'Look at this,' she said, ignoring the apology and holding up a pale green booklet. I went over to see it. It was my mother's old registration certificate. On the inside of its age-softened front cover was my mother's photograph: an unsmiling, rather wan 35-year-old, with prematurely greying hair and coffee-brown circles around her eyes. 'Hmm,' Monika said, looking over my shoulder. 'Never very big on grooming, was she?'

When my mother first came to England in 1937, she was classified as an Alien. Then, when the war broke out, she became an Enemy Alien, which meant, among other things, that if she wanted to travel outside Totnes, even for a day, she was required to go to the local police station two weeks in advance of her intended journey and ask permission. Such requests – along with the magnanimous responses – were all recorded in this little book. I flicked through the pages of stamps and hand-written comments ('Mrs Muller to Harwich for two days. Purpose of visit: shopping and to see friends. Permission granted'). I often accompanied my mother on her supplication visits to the Totnes police station. We would sit opposite the front desk, on the worn wooden 'Visitors' Bench', waiting until some gormless member of the Devonshire Constabulary could tear himself away from his busy crime-fighting schedule and attend to us in the Interview Room. The police didn't like my mother – she was the Hun, after all – and they always kept her hanging around, sometimes for hours at a time. Had she been prepared to joke or flirt or even get angry with the constables, she might have made things easier for herself. But she was not that sort of woman. My mother despised all admissions of hurt, whether from others or herself.

Monika pointed out a note near the end of the book, dated 1942, recording my mother's alteration of status to 'Refugee from Nazi Oppression'. 'God!' Monika said, laughing. 'I remember the day she came back from London with that – she was terribly angry because she didn't want to be known as a refugee.'

I closed the book and set it down on the coffee table.

'Would you like to keep that?' Monika asked.

'No.'

She shook her head. 'Willy, you have no sense of the past.'

'On the contrary. I have too much.'

'Whatever you say, darling.'

She had turned back to the chest of drawers now. I stood watching her as she riffled through the clutter. 'What do you want me to do?' I asked.

'Oh, I don't know,' she muttered. 'You could go through those papers over there on the recliner.'

I realized with a zing of irritation that Monika didn't really want me to do anything. When she had insisted, the night before, on having my help, she hadn't meant *help* in the practical sense of aid or succour. What she had really been asking for was my presence – someone to bear witness to her labour.

I went and got the pile of papers and sat down with it on the sofa. There was only rubbish here – ancient warranties for household appliances, mail-order catalogues for powdered vitamin supplements, yellowing newspaper advertisements for heating pads. As I sat, obediently sorting through the dreck, Monika chatted at me.

'Did I ever tell you what *Mutti* said when I got married to Lawrence?' (That was Monika's first husband – a fish-eyed hotel manager who turned out to be a wife-beater.) 'I was trying on my wedding dress for her. I was all excited and happy. She looked at me and said, "I suppose you know what to expect on your wedding night, don't you?" I was twenty-five! She thought I was a virgin! Can you imagine?'

I nodded absently. In between an old electricity bill and a recipe for lentil burgers cut out from *Health Times*, I had come upon a child's drawing executed in purple crayon. It was of a purple house with a purple, smoking chimney and four large, purple windows. In the upper right-hand corner of the page, just beneath a small, spiky, purple sun, the child had written, *Für Mutti. Leibe, Wilhelm.*

Monika was still talking. '*Mutti* hated sex, you know. She practically told me so, but it was obvious anyway that

153

she was frigid, just from the way she talked in general. I think that was a lot of the reason she disliked me so much. She looked down on me because she knew I liked sex . . .'

I must have loved her, I thought. *She must have loved me.* You think you know who you were all your life, but you don't. You can't hold *Paradise Lost* in your head, so why should you be able to retain your entire existence to date? You forget things. You forget things. You have to. You make do with cribs. People ask you about other times in your life and you give them vague topic headings: 'Oh, I was unhappy as a child . . . My twenties were very wild . . . We had a bad marriage.' You have to use those précis, otherwise you would spend your life being a bore, like those people who think 'How are you?' is a real question and insist on giving detailed answers. The terrible thing, though, is that in the end you believe the cribs yourself. The past, in all its epic detail, gets lost. Years pass and pass until you simply don't know any more that you were once a boy who liked his mother enough to draw her a purple picture.

16

11 *November 1979*

*I went round to see Monika last night and ended up
staying over. I had told Michael to call me there, but he
didn't. I nearly told her, just to tell someone, but I didn't
because I couldn't be sure she would approve of the
abortion bit. I slept in Morty's room, which was sort of
creepy. Was feeling restless and sad, so I took a Klonapin
that Nial had given me – just a half of one at first,
carefully sawn in two with a pair of nail scissors – and
then, when sleep didn't come, the other half washed
down with a couple of draughts of Monika's night-time
cough syrup. If I was keeping the baby I wouldn't be able
to take that sort of stuff. I like the transparent, plastic
beakerlets they give you with cough syrup these days –
dolly houseware, with those mysterious abbreviations
that appear three quarters of the way up in ghostly,
raised print: 2 TBSP, 1 FL OZ, ADULT DOSE. It makes
me feel small and cossetted, as if, any minute, I might
hear someone tinkling up the hallway with a tray of juice
and chicken soup and chunky wet flannels to slop on my
brow. In the middle of the night the phone rang and
Monika came into my bedroom very annoyed and said
it's someone called Michael for you. I had been deep in
syrupy sleep. 'So,' he said, when I picked up the phone.
'What's happening?' He sounded drunk. 'What do you
mean, what's happening?' I said. 'It's three in the fucking
morning.' There was a pause, during which I could hear
bar-noise in the background. 'No fucking problem,' he*

said and rang off. When the phone rang again, I thought it was him calling to apologize. 'Yes?' I said. 'Er, yes,' Michael said in a slurred voice. 'Could you put me through to Eileen Mitchell's room, please?'

'Michael,' I said. 'You're speaking to me again, you bastard.'

There was a shocked pause and then he hung up. I can't believe it. I can't believe it. He is fucking someone else. Someone beautiful and skinny called Eileen. Who isn't pregnant.

I'm going to go back to LA this afternoon. Monika wanted me to stay another day so that I could go and visit Oona's and Sadie's graves with her, but I've decided that, on balance, it wouldn't be such a good idea. I've had quite enough morbidity and quite enough England for one week.

Yesterday, in the taxi coming back from my mother's, I passed what used to be the Duke of Wellington on a side street in Holland Park. It's a winebar now. A winebar called Rachel's, but I recognized it immediately. I almost cried out. A couple of blocks further on, I made the driver stop and I got out to walk back and take another look. The new ownership has tarted the place up quite a bit. It has a big glass front with ruched pink curtains and a blackboard out on the pavement, announcing a tapas menu. I probably wouldn't have gone in, but I glimpsed two women through the window, sitting at the bar drinking white wine, and something – some ancient reflex – propelled me through the door.

It was early evening and the place hadn't really got going yet. Apart from the women, there were just two other patrons – a fat old duffer drinking espresso and a pretty-boy with sticking-up hair, reading a newspaper on one of those Frenchified reading sticks. I sat down at the bar. In a flush of nostalgia, I ordered a double Scotch. The two women glanced round at me as I was ordering, but when I smiled they scowled and resumed their whispered conference. I caught myself in the mirror behind the bar, just as my fangy, come-hither grin was fading. *Oh Christ.* The barman – some apple-cheeked little fucker – got my order wrong, of course. A thimble of Johnny Walker with no ice. I drank it anyway. Then another. Then another.

Presently, I got up to take a pee. They've put a new urinal and *toile de jouy* wallpaper in the men's. God . . . Now, who? . . . That time . . . *Oh the tiles are cold I've wanted to do this for ages I really have I've always fancied you.* Who was she . . . Janice? Geary and Lamming outside: *Come on, Muller, we need a slash!* Lois? And her mouth on me, all hot and dark. *Fuck off you piss artists, I'm busy!* And her frantic down there on the tiles updown updown downup, *sklosh, sklosh, sklosh* . . . Was it Maris? Maris! Welsh girl. And me looking down at her middle parting, wide and greyish white, like a lonely track in the forest, discovered from a plane . . .

God, there were a lot of women in those days. A lot. What was all that about? No, no, I mean, I know what it was *about*. But really. When I think of it now – all the names and numbers, and the sad single-girl flats with tattered bits of batik on the walls, and the rushing around in cabs and the bad lies – Oh-no-I've-got-a-deadline-I've-got-to-meet-Harry - the - car - broke - down - Samantha - is - my - research-assistant-if-you-don't-mind – when I remember all that, I think, How . . . *unnecessary.* Always, after we'd done fighting, Oona would say, *I can't even be angry, Willy. I don't hate you. I pity you. You don't know how to make yourself happy. How can I be angry?*

Who was that Frog writer who said he'd fucked one thousand women? I mean, what was his game? Did *he* know how to make himself happy?

When I got back to my hotel room, I climbed into bed

and snoozed for a bit. Penny arrived at around seven, all riled up from a day of witnessing her girlfriend's married bliss with a stockbroker in Chipping fucking Sodbury. She insisted on joining me in bed and kept laying her head on my chest, obscuring my view of the TV screen. After half an hour of listening to her yammer on resentfully about Laura Ashley bedspreads, I gave in and took her out for dinner.

We got a cab to a place in Soho that the concierge had recommended – a big barn of a restaurant called Smithie's on Old Compton Street. Oh! What a shithole! It was lit like a football stadium and filled with very young people who looked and dressed just like Heidi. The noise was almost unbearable. I wanted to leave as soon as we got there, but Penny, horrified at the prospect of failure, was determined to stay. 'This is fun,' she bravely insisted as we were led to our poorly situated table. Next to us, a couple were coming to the end of their meal. The young lady had on a tee-shirt made of plastic. They both looked up at the alien sound of Penny's optimistic trill and exchanged quick looks of sneering amusement.

'Come on, let's go,' I pleaded.

Penny made tutting noises and opened up her jewelled evening purse for a lipstick touch-up. 'Honeeey! Cool it, would you? You didn't even give the place a chance, yet.'

The food at Smithie's was shockingly nasty. We weren't allowed to choose our own dishes – we had to take what the kitchen had prepared that night. This, according to the waitress, was part of the restaurant's bid to revive the pleasures of authentic English tavern eating. By the words 'authentic' and 'English' and 'pleasures', I took her to mean roast beef, roast potatoes and so forth. But this was not the case. For hors d'oeuvres, Penny and I were presented with a plate of tripe and onions to share. After we had sent that away untouched, Penny received a dish of pig's trotters and lentils and I got an arrangement of parsnips and swedes entitled 'Old English Vegetable Plate'. We didn't stay for dessert (suet pudding and custard) and we only had two glasses of wine, but the bill, including service, came to £130.63.

Afterwards, as we were walking down Wardour Street looking for a cab, I met Michael Glynn, a journalist whom I used to work with on 24/7. He was coming from the opposite direction with an older woman in big red-framed glasses. There was that split second between mutual recognition and greeting, during which both of us had time to consider escape and to register, with a tinge of hurt, that the other party was considering the same thing. Then we donned amazed smiles and gave in to the inevitable.

'Willy!'

'Mike!'

'God! How . . . What are you doing here?'

'Just visiting for a couple of days. Sorry, this is Penny Vale. Penny, this is Mike, an old colleague of mine.'

'Hello. This is Amanda . . . you remember Amanda, Willy.'

I stared at the grey-haired crone in amazement. This was Amanda? Amanda with the legs and the eyes? Amanda who used to wear little skirts and her hair in two plaits? She was the same age as Oona. They used to pal around together. What happens to women?

'Yes, of course! Hello, Amanda.'

Amanda nodded a prune-faced hello. Oh, she remembered *me*.

'So . . .' Michael dug his hands in his pockets. 'How are things? What're you up to these days?'

'Oh this and that . . . and you?'

'Still in TV. I'm working for the BBC now – *Departures*? The documentary series? Now, wait a sec, didn't I read somewhere that you'd made a movie?'

'No, no . . . nothing's made . . .' Amanda's lips were growing thinner before my eyes.

'Oh, Willy!' Penny prodded me playfully. 'You're so modest! He's made a really big deal with Curzon to adapt his book. *To Have and to Hold*? Yeah, Hans Stempel is going to direct . . .'

'Great, great . . .' Michael glanced uncomfortably at his wife. 'Actually, I hate to rush off, but we're late to meet friends . . .'

'Of course, of course,' I said, stepping aside. 'It was nice to run into you.'

'Yes, very nice.' Michael put out his hand to shake and then, thinking better of it, changed the gesture to a farewell tap on my arm.

'Lovely. Good to see you, Willy. Nice to meet you, er, Polly . . .'

And with that, the two of them walked away, tripping slightly in their awkwardness.

I hate England. I hate everyone I used to know. I especially hate London. They could nuke it tomorrow and I would dance a flamenco on its glowing green ashes.

17

13 November 1979

*Went in again today. Same procedure. Same people. Got
the Valium, sat there in my little surgical dress and then I
got up, got dressed again. What are you doing, the nurse
said. I've changed my mind, I said. I think you should
speak to one of the counsellors, she said. Fuck the
fucking counsellors, I said. Had to wait half an hour for
a bus. On the way home, I called Michael at work. I am
having it, I told him. He said calm down, calm down,
you're being mad. I could tell he was really scared. But I
am calm, I said. He started talking very fast. He was
talking in this very odd way, using words he never
normally does. Like 'utterly'. You are being utterly
selfish. What about the child? Don't you know, children
need their fathers? I won't be depriving anyone of a
father, I said – that's your department. He hung up on
me. Then I called him back and I told him he had a
bloody cheek and he started really bellowing. He said I
was a very silly, silly little girl who didn't know the first
thing. Then he hung up again. Fuck him.*

Art's assistant, who was in charge of arranging our tickets
back to Mexico, messed up – *quelle surprise* – and what
was meant to be a one-day stopover in LA has turned into
four days. Art said he'd make it up to me by taking me to
lunch today, but when I turned up at his office he announced
that his father, Herb, would be joining us and that our
destination was no longer the Polo Lounge but some shit-

hole favourite of Herb's. We argued about this for a bit. Then we went to pick Herb up at his rest home in Cheviot Hills. Herb is eighty-nine now, and he has reached that stage in life when a man begins his metamorphosis into an earthworm. It took approximately five minutes for Art to get him from the front door to the car. I sat in the back seat, watching the two of them shuffle down the path – Herb, shakey and straight-legged like an old-fashioned monster, Art muttering gentle encouragement. 'That's it . . . there you go . . . mind the bump . . . good . . . we're nearly there . . .'

Art loves his father. It's a source of sorrow and some shame to him that Herb resides in a 'facility'. When Art's mother died and Herb moved out to Los Angeles from Florida, Art wanted him to come and live at his house, but Shirley, Art's wife – known to Art's friends as Shirley the Shark – would not hear of it. Art was outraged by this lack of family feeling. But I tend to Shirley's point of view on this one. What reasonable person would welcome the burden of Herb into their home?

Herb was finally levered into the car, bringing with him a miasma of baby powder, sour milk, sloppy hygiene: the smell of old person.

'Daddy, this is Willy,' Art said, getting in the other side. 'Remember Willy?'

'Hi there, Herb!' I said.

Herb twisted round slowly to study me. 'I dunno this guy,' he said roughly, turning back to Art.

'Willy's a good friend – that's all you need to know,' Art said.

'And he pays your son ten per cent of everything he earns,' I added.

Art gargled with mirth.

For lunch, Art had chosen a miserable deli on Wilshire Boulevard in Santa Monica. 'Daddy likes it,' he explained when I objected. Inside, the restaurant was dark and smelled of some sort of cooking oil that made me nauseous. We sat down in a red plastic booth at the front – Art and Herb on one side, me on the other, facing the crazy, two-man panel.

'Daddy? What do you want to eat, Daddy?' Art asked, holding up the laminated concertina menu before his father's blinking face. 'You want to have the brisket? Or the stuffed cabbage?'

'Knockwurst,' Herb gasped.

'You sure?' Art asked.

'With beans,' Herb added. 'And matzoh ball soup to start.'

Art smiled at me. 'He's pretty happy today. The Yankees won. Didn't they, Daddy? The Yankees won, didn't they?' Herb's face lit up momentarily, and he nodded furiously. 'It was a good game, right?' Art pressed. 'It was a good game?' There was more nodding. I saw several flakes of dandruff drift from the old man's wispy white locks on to the formica table. *Oh, for God's sake.*

The waitress came over – a grey-haired gargoyle with varicose veins throbbing beneath her tan-coloured stockings. Art ordered knockwurst and cream sodas for him and his father. I asked for a black coffee.

'So, how was London?' Art asked, as the waitress retreated.

'Ach, you know. Not great.'

'Did you get my flowers?' Art asked. 'I sent flowers.'

'Yes, we did. That was a very kind thought, Art. I appreciate it.'

Art shrugged. 'It was the least' – he lowered his voice so that his father would not hear – 'I know what it is to lose a mother.'

The waitress returned now, with the coffee and soda and four orange plastic tumblers of tap-water. A woman sitting facing me in the next booth was talking loudly about some baroque family troubles.

'I said to him, "Parker, if you do any more of that, she's gonna get the cops on to you." He says, "Aw, don't worry, Ma." And I'm like . . . "Whatever."'

'So how has the work been going?' Art asked me.

I tried not to scowl. 'Well, you know, it's hard . . .'

'Yeah, yeah. I know,' Art said impatiently. 'Everything's hard. But are you getting something done?'

'Sure. I'm working. I saw the Kraut by the way.'

'Oh yes? And what's he like?'

'Unbearable. Swans around this mo place of his . . .'

'He's a mo?'

'No, he just lives that way. Art, I'm telling you, you should have seen his house . . .'

'But you're getting the work done.'

'Yes. Yes. It's just tricky, you know, coming back to all this stuff, after all this time.'

Art took a long draught of soda. 'I know,' he said, his voice turning misty. 'Makes you miss her, doesn't it?' He reached his hand out across the table and settled it plumply on mine. I hastily pulled my hand back. 'Frankly, Art, no. It doesn't.'

If there is one thing I want to discuss less with Art than how my work is going, it is Oona. Art has always persisted in the illusion that Oona's and mine was a great but tragic love. It is part of his sentimental nature to believe that all loves are great and tragic. No doubt when Shirley the Shark dies, Art will weep and rage over her portly corpse, like Antony over Cleopatra.

'It's okay,' Art murmured now, registering my reluctance. 'I know it hurts.'

The woman in the next booth was still talking about her son.

'I told him, "Look, you made a bad marriage, now you gotta live with it. That's life." He knows it, though. He's

a good boy. He's got a good heart, hasn't he? Don't you think?'

The other party on the opposite side of the booth said something in reply that I couldn't make out. It evidently displeased Parker's mother.

'Well! Very nice, Mr Sheiss! That's a lovely thing to say! A lovely thing to say to me!'

The food arrived. Herb squeezed a great quantity of ketchup into his matzoh ball soup, then mashed up the matzoh and began to ferry spoonfuls of the resulting pink goo into his gummy maw. Art, meanwhile, was sawing up his knockwurst into large violet spheres.

'So, did you do anything else while you were in London?' he asked, with his mouth full.

'No, not much,' I said, studiously averting my gaze. 'I went to see Sophie . . .'

'No kidding?' Art exclaimed. I felt a fleck of projectile wurst hit my neck. 'That's great, Willy. That's really great. I'm so happy for you. You know what? I've actually been thinking of fixing something up with *Hey There!* magazine – a little feature about you and the movie. But this is so much more perfect. They could do a whole Muller Family Reunited thing – they'd take that in a second. And they pay, you know . . .'

'Er, no,' I interrupted. 'That is not going to work . . .' I looked at Art sweating and snuffling over his food. 'Art, can I tell you? If you're going to eat stuff that's bad for you, why don't you make it something worthwhile? You're using up a week's worth of recommended fat intake on that piece of shit on your plate . . .'

'Ach, shut up,' Art said cheerfully. 'Me and Daddy like our simple food. Don't we, Daddy?'

Herb grunted.

'Now, look,' Art continued. 'Don't say yes or no right now to the *Hey There!* piece. Think about it first . . . Daddy, you want some more of that? Or you want to have your knockwurst now?'

'No, Art, you don't understand,' I said.

'Wurst,' Herb announced. Art pushed the soup bowl away and replaced it with the sausage plate.

'I couldn't do a reunited story,' I said, 'because no one has reunited. Sophie only wanted to see me to ponce money for her and her drug-addict boyfriend.'

'And did she succeed?' Art asked.

'What?'

'Did you give her money?'

I sighed. 'Yes. Yes, I did . . .'

'Well, Willy, are you crazy?'

'Yes, probably . . . Look, I don't want to put a dampener on this lovely family gathering, Art, but if I stay in this place a minute longer I'm going to slit my wrists.'

There was a pause while Art chewed and swallowed.

'Hello?' he said, finally. 'You haven't even finished your lousy frigging coffee. Relax, will you? What the fuck is the matter with you?'

'Oh, let's see. My mother just died. My daughter killed herself . . .'

'Oh, Christ, Willy,' Art interrupted. 'You're so full of self-pity.'

'Well, someone's got to do it.'

'Do what?'

'Pity me, for Christ's sake.'

Art put down his knife and fork. 'No they don't, Willy. That's just where you're wrong. No one's got to do anything but live their life, eat their chicken and peas, and die.'

After we had finished lunch and dropped Herb back at the home, we drove back to where my car was parked and I set off for Calabasas to see my business manager, Meir

Rosenblatt. Last year, on his seventieth birthday, Rosenblatt officially retired, but he has maintained a select group of clients whom he now receives at his home. This is not the most convenient arrangement for me, but I have been too lazy, so far, to set about finding someone else. In any case, I quite enjoy these little visits.

When I turned up, his fabulously desiccated wife, Cynthia, was standing in the driveway overseeing a squad of Mexican men as they attempted to coax the parched Rosenblatt flowerbeds into bloom. She had just returned from a lunch appointment and was wearing a very tight, very rigid, coral-coloured skirt suit and matching pumps with little bows on the front. I could hear her screeching at the gardeners before I got out of the car.

'No!' she was saying, flapping her hands in a despairing gesture. 'Not like that! I want the roses in a profusion!' On catching sight of me, her scowl melted into an expression of droop-eyed gentility. 'Oh, Mr Muller! How nice to see you!' Her hair was standing high on her little peanut head, stiff and purple-brown. Her face appeared to be sagging beneath the weight of her make-up: lipstick was bleeding into a dozen little channels around her mouth, and in the cross-hatching of her wrinkles some terrible khaki-coloured emulsion had settled like silt. Standing there in the bright sunlight, she was almost heroic in her hideousness.

She turned and led me past the white plaster columns of the porch into the marbled, chandeliered hallway. 'I'll just go and let him know that you're here,' Cynthia said. I stood around examining some glass figurines arranged on a plinth and shivering in my short sleeves. The Rosenblatts are big fans of air conditioning. Even on a hot day it's cold enough to hang meat in their house. On the hallway loveseat I noticed a new pillow – one of those needlepoint things they sell in boutiques on Montana Avenue. This one bore the legend, 'I can resist anything . . . but chocolate!'

Presently, Cynthia returned and took me out to Meir in the garden. Last year, after a decade of monstrously expensive efforts to transform her back yard into an English lawn, Cynthia gave up and had Astroturf installed. The result is rather pleasant in a surreal sort of way – like a great, spikey, outdoor carpet. Meir was sitting reading, under a lemon tree at the far end of the garden, surrounded by a vast amount of very new, very fancy, outdoor furniture. As I crunched my way over to him, he put down his book and waved.

'Hello, cookie! How was your trip to England?'

I picked out a chair and sat down. 'It was okay . . .'

'One second.' Meir held up his hand. 'Cynthia – could you tell Concepción to bring some more iced tea? Thank you.' He turned back to me. 'Listen, cookie, I was sorry to hear about your mother.'

'Yeah, well. She'd had a good innings . . . What's with all the furniture, Meir? You thinking of having a garden party?'

He shook his head hopelessly. 'It's Cynthia. She spends like I can't tell you. The other day it was three thousand dollars on sheets. *Sheets*. I tell her, "Cynthia, dulling, we are not maharajahs." But it makes no difference. We will end up out on the street . . . So, okay now, tell me more about London, cookie. Was it swinging like a pendulum do?'

'Not really.'

'Who did you see?'

'Well, I saw my daughter.'

Meir's eyes widened. He knows a little about my family situation.

'No!' he said.

'Yes.'

'How long has it been?'

'Nine years.'

'So how was it?'

'Not so good. She lives on a council estate – you know, like a project. Her boyfriend's a drug addict.'

Meir made guttural noises of horror and sympathy.

Encouraged, I began to lay it on thick. 'She has a six-year-old son who sees a psychiatrist. She took money from me and then she called me a murderer.'

Meir's face was quite contorted now with indignation. 'How much?' he whispered.

'Oh, not so much. Three hundred.'

'Pounds or dollars?'

'Pounds.'

Meir sat up in his chair. 'God! Kids! You know, Sarah says she wants to go to law school, now. Another half a million like that' – he clicked his fingers – 'because all of a sudden she doesn't like dentistry! I said to her, "Cookie, you're not meant to like it, you're meant to make money at it." But this is America!'

Meir has a couple of hobby-horses. One has to do with the restorative powers of dried orange peel in a hot bath. The other – the one he's really passionate about – is child-rearing methods in modern America. I settled back in my deck-chair, preparing myself for a long blast.

'It's all about what the parents owe the kids!' he said. 'People go to see *King Lear* now – you think they understand what is going on? Of course not! They're amazed the daughters put up with the old man for so long. "Oh, poor Gonerill, she's got such an old shitty bitty for a dad . . ." And why? Why this reaction? Because the whole concept of a child's duty to the parents is gone now – extinct! When I was a boy, I was working as a delivery boy – delivering groceries five nights a week, and giving the money to my mother. From the age of thirteen! Yes! And you know what? If Sarah can support herself by the age of thirty it will be a miracle!'

Ah yes, but, for all your bitching, you do support her. What do I do? I fuck off to America – return once a decade to throw guilt money at my daughter and then scarper. It is the familiar pattern of my conversations with Meir: I will complain about something – some wrong done to me – and he will leap to my vociferous defence. Then, while elaborating on my blamelessness, he will manage, somehow, to plant doubts in my mind. I've never known whether to attribute this to tactlessness or some unconscious enmity on his part.

'Well, Willy, I should tell you,' he said now, 'this is no time for you to be giving away money.'

'Oh?' I smiled. I make it a point never to betray anxiety about financial matters, particularly to my financial advisers.

'No, cookie, don't play now. I'm serious. You're in bad shape.'

'Aw, come on. How bad can it be?'

'You have $200,000 owing in federal back taxes. How bad is that?'

'I see.'

'And this crazy Mexican place – I don't know what you're doing there. This is a place that Steven Spielberg should be renting, not you.'

'Okay, when the movie gets made, I'll . . .'

'Willy, please. When we see the pigs flying.'

'So what are you saying?'

'I'm saying you have to make cut-backs. Maybe sell the house.'

We sat in silence.

'Meir, let me ask you something,' I said after a while.

'Sure.'

'Do you think I'm a bad person?'

'Only God knows that for sure, Willy.'

'So you don't have an opinion at all?'

'Not one that really matters.'

'Okay, let me ask you something else. If the Polish peasant who hid Jews from the Nazis is a hero, what is the Polish peasant who turned the Jews away? Is he a coward?'

Meir smiled. 'Of course.'

'Really? A coward? A bad man?'

'A coward isn't a bad man, necessarily. You can't know if you're a bad man until you die.'

'You've got to wait until you hear God's decision?'

'Well, yes, that's true. But I meant something else. Only when you die do you run out of chances to be good. Until then, there is always the possibility of turning yourself around.'

18

16 December 1979

Sick as a dog this morning. Nearly puked on the bus to work. My hair has gone funny, which is to do with the hormones. Tonight I went to see S and N. Sophie is very narky with me about being pregnant – says I am stupid to have a baby on my own. I think she just hates the idea of me doing something unconventional that she hasn't done. Just like when I was seeing Dr Robbo – she got all snotty because she wanted the monopoly on interesting psychological conditions. She told Monika, when I had expressly told her not to, so I suppose I will be getting a phone call soon. Jack was at his friend's house tonight, so me, Sophie and Nial went to the pub. Nial got talking to this scuzzy old man called Heinz who claimed to be a graphologist, and he ended up giving us all a reading. Sophie, who was quite stoned, wrote, 'Somewhere over the rainbow, skys are blue,' as her sample sentence. Heinz told her she was impatient and very intelligent and creative. Also, the big loops of her ls indicated a 'strong erotic drive'. (Translation: Heinz wanted to fuck her.) Nial took ages to write his sentence – some pretentious thing about heroin. Heinz pored over it for a long time before shaking his head and declaring Nial's handwriting uninterpretable. I think he saw madness in it and didn't want to say. Nial took umbrage and staggered off to play darts. Then I wrote, 'I have had a long day and I'm very tired', but Heinz seemed to have lost interest in graphology by this point. He muttered something cursory about my having open and generous es and ts but very anxious serifs, and then he started stroking Sophie's hair.

Penny and I left Los Angeles on Saturday night. To make up for his assistant's incompetence, Art had very sweetly arranged cheap business-class seats for us through some relation of his who works for Air Mexico. (As always when Art performs these miracles, my gratitude was blunted by a vague irritation with the seeming arbitrariness of his beneficence: why had he waited until now to pull these strings?) The connecting flight at Mexico City left on time, and we arrived in Puerto Vallarta at six on Sunday morning. Harry, needless to say, was not at the airport as promised, so we took a cab in.

I was standing in the driveway of the villa, rootling in my jacket pocket for keys, when I noticed that the front door of the house was ajar. I left Penny to pay the driver and went in. 'Harry, you drunken fuck,' I was shouting as I crossed the threshold. 'You left the fucking door . . .' I stopped mid-sentence, arrested by the sight of Sissy Yerxa's Limoges vase lying in three large shards on the hall floor. Stepping across them, I entered the living room. It smelled odd. It smelled *bad*. But everything seemed more or less as I had left it. *Fuck it. One broken vase and he stunk up the place a little – it could have been worse.* I turned to go out and help Penny bring in the bags. As I did so, something on the far side of the room caught my eye. I knew immediately what it was, but, hoping, vainly, to be proved wrong, I moved closer to inspect. Sure enough, coiled quietly on the middle cushion of Sissy Yerxa's white sofa, was a large, impressively fibrous, human turd.

Upstairs, I woke Harry with a glass of water over his head.

'Wake up, you bastard! You fucker!'

Harry rolled over and gazed at me. 'Please stop that,' he said in a suffering tone.

'What the fuck were you thinking? I'm going to fucking kill you, you fuck!'

Harry laid a finger to his lips: 'Shhhh'.

'I've had it with you, Harry!'

Harry slowly sat up. 'Look, Muller, I really am going to have to insist that you lower the volume a bit.'

Downstairs, I heard the front door slam and then, a few seconds later, a shrill little cry of distress. Penny had evidently met the turd. I lost control now, and began trying to drag Harry out of bed. Given our relative sizes and weights, this was a rather pathetic effort. For a time, Harry lay impassively as I tore at his bedclothes and pummelled at his chest. Then, finally, with a lazy sort of reluctance, he punched me. I swerved, so that it only caught me on the bicep, but that was enough. It was one of those blows that send a shivery streak of pain through the entire body. There was silence in the room as I crouched by the nightstand, nursing my right arm with my left. 'Sorry, Muller,' Harry said. 'I just can't bear a hysteric. Not in the morning.'

I staggered into a standing position. 'You fuck . . . you fucking fuck . . .' I was, I realized, close to tears.

Penny came clattering up the stairs now. 'Oh my God,' she exclaimed as she entered the room. 'Oh my God. I am so . . . Did you call the police, Willy?'

I let out a yowl of frustration at her stupidity. 'What, you think they're going to arrest him for shitting on the sofa?'

Penny looked at Harry and then back at me in confusion. 'What are you talking about, babe? We've been *burgled*.'

Every friendship has its breaking point. For even the strongest, oldest platonic unions, there is some level of pressure or abuse that proves insupportable. The look on Harry's hungover face, as it slowly dawned on him that I had been accusing him of defecating on Sissy Yerxa's sofa, indicated that just such a moment had arrived in our relationship. God knows why. Mine wasn't such an outrageous assumption – he did wet his bed after all. But then, that's the thing about breaking points – you rarely know what they're going to be until you arrive at them. You'll fret and faff for weeks about stealing your chum's girlfriend, only to meet him in the street and have him clap you on the back and laugh admiringly at your cheek. Then, another day, you'll rib him comfortably about his art collection, and without warning you're cast out for ever.

'Christ,' I said. 'I'm sorry, Harry, I . . .'

He waved me off with a dry chuckle. His lips were pursed. His cheeks were flushed. 'That's all right, old man,' he said, avoiding my eyes. 'No offence taken.'

I went downstairs to call the police. Standing outside on the veranda (the living room was too malodorous), I struggled for about fifteen minutes to explain to a sleepy-sounding Mexican cop that I had been robbed. He could not, or would not, understand my pidgin Spanish, and eventually he hung up on me. Fortunately, Julia the cook arrived at this point, and after some protracted sign-language negotiation I got her to call the police station back.

In the meantime, Penny, with the happy outrage that possesses a certain kind of woman in moments of crisis, had been going through the villa making an inventory of missing items. Our robber friends had restricted themselves, it seemed, to the ground floor of the villa. As far as Penny could ascertain, their haul had comprised the music system, the television, a triptych of woven wall-hangings, some porcelain knick-knacks and four silver candlesticks. A pretty lousy haul, really – the dopes.

When Julia got off the phone, Penny insisted I call Sissy Yerxa, pointing out that since Sissy was going to find out about the burglary sooner or later, it would be good form to let her know immediately. Sissy wasn't picking up so I got away with leaving a message on her machine; I kept it short and as non-alarmist as possible.

'Sissy? Good morning. It's Willy Muller here. Sorry to bother you this early, but it appears we've had a small break-in at the house. We've informed the police, everything's under control. I'll call later to let you know what's going on.'

I was just going into the kitchen to get Julia to make me a papaya shake for breakfast when Harry came down the stairs in his bathrobe. 'Good God!' he said when he saw the turd. 'That robber must have a first-rate colon. I haven't produced a specimen like that in twenty years.'

I laughed – a little too eagerly, perhaps. Harry shot me a cold look. He truffled about the living room in silence for a bit. Then he announced that his passport was missing.

He had gone back upstairs by the time the police arrived half an hour later. There were three of them – three skinny machos with moustaches and hot, dark uniforms and guns. They clanked as they moved. They asked me a few questions, using Julia as a translator, then they started wandering around the living room, talking quietly amongst themselves. I was rather flattered to see how gravely the police were taking my little calamity, but Penny was bursting with customer dissatisfaction. 'Hey, aren't they going to take fingerprints?' she wanted to know. 'They've got to take fingerprints! Julia – fingerprintay, no?' Julia shrugged. The police were now standing in a solemn semi-circle, gazing down at the turd. 'Are they just going to stand there, looking at it?' Penny hissed. 'Shouldn't they take a sample for, like, forensics?'

The phone rang and Penny ran to answer it.

'That was Hans,' she said when she came back. 'He's coming over.'

I clasped my forehead. 'What, Stempel? Here? Oh, God, *no*. Why?'

Penny put her hands on her hips. 'Hey, you, don't be mean. He only wants to help.'

'That's ridiculous!' I said. 'There's nothing for him to do. I don't want him here.'

Penny came over and stroked my head. 'Honey, it'll be good to have him here. He speaks Spanish.'

I swatted her hand away. 'Get off me.'

There was a sound in the hallway. Penny and I turned around to find Sissy Yerxa standing before us, with a piece of her shattered Limoges in her clenched fist.

'I got your message,' she said. 'I came at once . . . Oh, Jesus . . .' She was staring past us at the turd. 'What in God's name . . . ?' She began speaking very rapidly to the three policemen in Spanish. Penny and I stood silently as they rattled away at each other. At length, Sissy turned to me.

'How did this happen?' she said. Her tone was faintly accusatory. 'Didn't you have the alarm system on?'

I shrugged. 'Well, I've been out of town for a couple of days, so I . . .'

At this moment, Harry wandered downstairs again. He was still in his shaggy robe.

'Uh, you've met Harry, Sissy. He was actually the only one here last night.'

Sissy eyed Harry suspiciously. 'Did you have the alarm system on?'

Harry appeared not to hear the question. He stood at the foot of the staircase, gazing at the policemen with a slight frown. I could feel trouble coming on.

'Hello-o?' Sissy trilled impatiently.

Harry still didn't look at her. Finally, after five seconds of painful silence, he turned to me. 'Is this,' he said, waving in Sissy's direction, 'that bint who owns the place?'

'Excuuuse me?' Sissy said. 'What did you say?'

'What?' Harry turned to her with a sweet, flustered smile. 'Oh, sorry, I was just enquiring as to which coven you came from.'

Ah, so that was it. Harry was taking his revenge.

Sissy's eyes, which have a slightly bulging, thyroid look at the best of times, threatened now to leave her skull altogether.

'Listen, creep,' she screamed. 'This happens to be my house and I'll thank you not to insult me while you're in it.'

'Now, let's . . .' I began.

'Willy,' Harry interrupted, shaking his head. 'It seems this woman is *menstruating* or something. Can we send her away?'

During the row that ensued, Stempel turned up. 'Hi guys!' he said brightly, as he sauntered in. 'Hey! Something smells bad around here . . .' He paused, taking in the taut silence of the room.

'What's going on, people?' he said. He had immediately adopted a revolting, Jesus-arbitrating-among-the-Nazarenes tone.

'You keep out of it, Kraut!' Harry roared.

Penny pushed Harry angrily. 'Lookit, Harry, you're totally out of line!'

'Hans, this man has been insulting me . . .' Sissy whimpered.

Harry put his hands over his eyes. 'Christ! Fucking wenches!' he moaned. Then Sissy spat at him.

The act of spitting is fascinating to me. Who thought of it first? I've only been spat at once. It happened in court, at the end of the first trial, just after the jury foreman – the jury forewoman, actually – had pronounced the guilty verdict. *Why doesn't she like me?* I remember thinking, in a moment of madness. Then there was a great blur of faces as I was trooped back downstairs to my cell and I heard Oona's mother Sibella cry out, in the sweetly inept way of someone not used to swearing, 'You bloody, bloody man.' Then something silvery shot through the air. Spit. It seemed such a thrillingly primitive thing for her to do. Amid the swimming-pool roar of the courtroom, I heard the tiny, satisfying *flurp* as it hit the floor behind me.

Sissy was a better aim than Sibella. Hers landed on Harry's robe. Harry shouted something and moved towards her with the apparent intention of hitting her. But whether or not he succeeded in doing this, I don't know, because at that moment, with rather brilliant dramatic timing, I passed out.

19

27 May 1980

*I am ENORMOUS right now. Not just my belly.
Everything has grown vast and quivery. I could weep.
Everyone said I would start to glow after the first
trimester, but I am obviously not the glowing sort. Even
Nial looks healthy next to me. Aunt Monika said I
couldn't have the baby when I was still in the squat, so
I've moved in with her until the council gives me a flat. It
is lovely to be somewhere civilized but it's a bit of a
strain living with Monika. She is always trying to force
food down me and going on at me about sorting myself
out. She thinks I should go after Michael for child
support. When I told her Michael was married she just
said, 'Oh, I assumed that.' She's not stupid. Last week I
went with Sophie to buy clothes and stuff and I had a bit
of a freak-out. It's not the thought of the baby so much
as the other things. Who's going to ever go to bed with
me when I have a kid? Mum had Sophie when she was
twenty-three and she always used to say that that was
too early. She said no woman should have kids until she
is forty, because at that age you don't mind staying in so
much. The woman in the baby shop showed us this
gadget that eats up dirty nappies and ejects them in a
perfect, non-stinky ball. Sophie said she would buy me
one when she gets some money. She was thrilled by it.
Perhaps you have to be a mother.*

Well.

Naturally, the assumption when I fell down on Sissy's living-room floor was that I was having another heart attack. I came to after only a few seconds (just in time to prevent one of the Mexican policemen from administering mouth-to-mouth), but Penny went ahead and called an ambulance anyway. Within minutes I was being borne away on a gurney by two strapping blond guys with fat red crosses on their sleeves.

I have been 'under observation' in the Weismann wing of the PV AmeriClinic for two days now, and I must say, it's really not bad here. My room is clean and the nurses don't speak enough English to be capable of bugging me. Disappointingly, I appear to be just fine. They've done every kind of check on me and the worst diagnosis they can come up with is dehydration and exhaustion. The doctor told me this morning that I can leave tomorrow, as long as I promise to get bed-rest for at least seven days, blah blah.

Harry is leaving this afternoon. He has to go to Mexico City to get a temporary passport from the British Consulate and then he'll be heading back to London. He came in to the hospital earlier, to say goodbye, and I tried joking with him about stuff, but he was very quiet and grave. Just before he left, I made some jovial reference to my health problems, and he gave a mean little twisted smile.

'Yes, yes, poor Willy,' he muttered, staring at the floor. 'Always more sinned against than sinning.'

I asked him what he meant by that, but he wouldn't say. The big baby.

After Harry left, Penny came in and we had an argument. Sissy has apparently 'had it' with me and my loutish friends. She is demanding that I vacate Casa De La Luna immediately. Penny seemed to think I could wrangle a reprieve if I got Art involved, but I told her I'd be fucked if I was going to give that skinny bitch the satisfaction. Then Penny brought up Stempel, who of course knows all about the heart attack now and has offered to put us up at his house if we have to leave Sissy's. Penny was slobberingly eager to accept this invitation, so when I told her that Stempel could go fuck himself, too, and that I'd rather sleep on the beach, she went into a sulk.

'Well, tell me, then,' she said after a long, pouty silence, 'where are we going to stay? Shall I book us a room at The Palm?'

I laughed. 'Are you mad? I can barely afford a Motel 6.'

Penny's dolly-nose crinkled slightly. She disapproves of men mentioning money – particularly their lack of it – in the presence of ladies.

'What are we going to do, then?' she asked. 'Because the reality is, Willy, if we don't say yes to Hans, we're out on the street.'

'We'll go back to LA,' I said. 'You can call and change the tickets when you get back tonight.'

'What?' she shouted. 'Don't be crazy, Willy. You're a sick man. You can't go flying off like that.'

'Penny . . .'

'You know something, Willy? You are not well, and if you go racing around like this you're going to die. Yes. I'm sorry, but this is the reality . . .'

'Penny, I will die if I stay at Stempel's.'

'Would you stop being so mean about Hans? Lookit, he's been nothing but sweet to us.'

'Uh-huh.'

'I mean it, Willy. Get over yourself for a second, would you? You can't fly to Los Angeles. The doctor says you need bed . . .'

'Please shut up! I can't bear any more of this! I'm going back to LA. If you want to stay and make nice with the Kraut, by all means go ahead.'

'Oh yeah?'

'Yeah.'

'Really.'

'Really.'

'Well, fine then. I will.'

Of course, she started crying at this point. 'I don't know why you always have to be so mean to me, Willy. Why you have to be such a pig . . .'

There are about two women in the world who look good when they're blubbing – and Penny isn't one of them. Her face inflates, her nose becomes bulbous. Also, this phlegmy thing starts going on with her voice. It's not pretty.

'I . . . I . . .' she went on. 'I've given you so much love and . . .'

I closed my eyes in anticipation of a long session, but almost immediately she broke off. She looked at me for a long time, her swollen little piggy face all solemn and severe. Then she kissed me lightly on the forehead and walked out of the room. Very affecting. I tremble to think what hellish making-up-is-hard-to-do scenes she has planned for the flight home tomorrow.

20

Pearl literally cried all night last night. I thought I was going to go mad. It's only been three weeks, but I feel like I've been doing this for five years. I am so exhausted all the time. I look like shit, too. I can't remember when I last brushed my hair. Monika said she called Dad to tell him he had a grand-daughter. Whoopee-doo. I took Pearl in for her shots yesterday and I was complaining about my sore breasts, so the nurse got the doctor to take a look. It was so soothing having some nice old man's soft, clean, hands patting kindly at my tits, I nearly cried. Pathetic. I thought that having my own flat would be a big relief, which it is in a lot of ways, but it is incredibly lonely. There were a couple of days last week when the only people I talked to were cashiers at the supermarket. Some of the girls from work have been to visit, but I think they found it – me – a bit depressing. Sophie's been over a few times, but it's always awful when she comes. She tells me I'm doing everything wrong and then, if I turn my back for one second, Jack is trying to poke something up Pearl's bum.

The idea of progression, of going in a line somewhere, seems to have fallen away. I never noticed it happening. Maybe it's just hard to find meaning in life without a boyfriend or the prospect of a boyfriend. Not that I've ever had a real boyfriend. And not that a boyfriend would be so meaningful. But it might blanket you from

*the void a bit. When I cry, I get a hollow pain in my
chest, just like in the songs.*

I've been back in LA almost a week now. *Is this it?* I keep
asking myself with a sort of anxious excitement, *Have I
reached the end of my tether? Am I mad yet?* Penny did not
come back with me, after all. When I was discharged from
the hospital, I found a single air ticket waiting for me at
the Casa De La Luna, along with a note.

Dear Babycakes,
I am very confused about our relationship right now. I
love you but I need time to think things over. I am going
to stay at Hans's place for a while. I'll see you back in
LA in a week or so.
Love ya, Penny

Or so. Week *or so*. Get her. I assume she and Stempel
are fucking. It seems a little impolitic of him given his
involvement with the movie, but then again, maybe he sees
shtupping my girlfriend as his droit du directorial seigneur.
He's probably cartwheeling her around his ugly fucking
casa as I speak. Well, fine. They can lie in those twin
bathtubs of his and bore each other to death. Inside the 'o'
of 'Love', Penny had drawn a smiley face. Idiot woman.
  Last night, at ten o'clock, I leaped up from the sofa and
started calling people. For an hour I flicked through my
address book, frantically seeking acquaintances with whom
I could feasibly arrange brunches, barbecues, tennis
doubles, drinks. But the burst of social enthusiasm evapor-
ated as rapidly as it came on. By midnight I was in bed,
watching TV and eating a rather disgusting but addictive
microwaved savoury called 'Hot Pockets'. At some point
during the night, I came awake with the TV still blaring

and Hot Pocket crumbs making grease marks on my sheets. Then, for hour after insufferable hour, I lay staring up at the ceiling, monitoring myself, writing myself little reviews on the ebb and flow of my dread.

Most of my fretting seems to be about money. Was Meir laying it on thick to frighten me? When do the bailiffs turn up? I've been poor before, God knows. But it's different when you're young. When Oona and I were first married, our joint annual income was £500. I was still at the *Herald* and Oona was working as an assistant to some old fart at London University. Oona once gave herself second degree burns scrabbling to retrieve a ten-shilling note she had mistakenly thrown into the fire while cleaning out the pockets of her father's old greatcoat. We lived in a rancid three-room flat in Mornington Crescent and ate soup that I made from chicken bones and vegetables bought at end-of-the-day prices from the Inverness Street market. (Oona knew how to cook only one dish, and that required large amounts of unaffordable cream and bacon.) We were still living in Mornington Crescent when Sophie was born. There is a picture, somewhere, of Oona and me standing on the street, just back from the hospital. Oona is carrying the baby-bundle. She has a swollen, blotchy face – I think she had a cold – and she's dressed in one of those beribboned sacks that expectant mothers used to wear. I am standing with my arm round her, looking preposterously young and self-conscious. What really strikes me about the picture is the mildness of our expressions. Perhaps I am misreading what is really only the asinine glow of youth. But in that picture we look . . . content. As if life in our little slum, with a new, squawling baby, is just peachy. Most of that has faded now, but I can remember some things – the mornings in particular: the crackly radio, the taste of cheap jam; Oona emerging naked from the bathroom, her wet hair in a turban, her arms out to receive the baby: *Did*

Daddy look after you while Mummy was in the bath? Oona used to read to me at night. Ha! Not whole books, just things from whatever she was reading to help me sleep. (I slept badly, even then.) Sometimes, I would put my head on her belly to feel the vibration of her words. Or else I would lie next to her, very close, so I could see the pale fur on her face, illuminated by the bedside lamp, or watch the grave back and forth of her eyes across the page.

At dawn this morning, I was out on the deck with a portable phone, cancelling the dates I made the previous evening. I paced back and forth across the splintered wooden planks, barking my regrets into answering machines across the sleeping city. By the time I was done the sky had turned that sad dawn-orange. If I have to sell this house, where will I go? One of those old apartment complexes in West Hollywood, with a communal swimming pool and dodgy shower heads? Do they let men of my age live in such places? I lay down on a recliner and wept for a short while. Then I got up and went to my study to write a letter.

21

12 April 1981

Something terrible has happened. I've done something so
wicked I'm scared to write it down. Last night, just after
I'd finished putting Pearl down, Nial turned up. He's
never been round before on his own. I thought something
was wrong, but he said, no, no, he was just looking in to
see if I was all right, which was crap but I didn't go on
about it. I let him in and made a cup of tea and he
laughed because I'd been in the middle of watching
Coronation Street. Not nastily though. He was a bit
stoned, but not very. More depressed. He asked could he
have a look at Pearl which was also weird but I let him
tiptoe in and have a look. And then he came out and we
had the tea and he asked was there anything to put in it,
and I got out some Bailey's that Monika gave me for
medicinal whatever. I think it was around then that I got
an idea maybe he was going to try something. There was
just this really funny atmosphere in the room and he kept
saying all these nice things like how well I looked (do
reckon) and how nicely I'd done the flat. I said to him
how's Soph and he goes oh, you know, same as ever. We
sat chatting for about an hour. He was sitting on this
sofa and I was sitting on this crappy little stool, and after
a bit he goes, Why don't you come and sit here and be
comfy? Honestly, I didn't want him to touch me but he
said it in such a sweet way and it was so nice to have a
man saying kind things. I went and sat down at the other
end, but its not that big, so we were only a couple of

inches apart. The telly was still on and we just sat there looking at it and then he kissed me. Oh God, it wasn't even nice when it was happening. He's got these big teeth and he was sort of biting as he kissed. I don't know why I didn't stop it, I don't fancy him. It was like I was standing in another part of the room watching it, and I'm like, Well, well, what are you up to now, girl? He was making a big noise, grunting and groaning – he really is a pretty disgusting bloke, but when they're so excited and panting and everything, you sort of get into it in spite of yourself. I kept thinking, This is Sophie's boyfriend, but I kept on doing it. And part of me was thinking, why would he have me, when he could have Sophie? And I thought maybe he's always liked me – people have types don't they and maybe I'm more his type. And then when he'd got his shirt off and my shirt off and his hand down my knickers, and I'm wondering about the broken veins on my breasts from having Pearl, he suddenly stops – sits up. This is wrong, he says. And I wanted to say, But now we've already been bad – we've crossed the line that makes us bad people – so can't we at least finish it? And then the next thing I'm thinking, oh God, he stopped it. I was about to fuck my sister's boyfriend and it took him to stop it. 'You're right,' I said. 'You should leave now and we'll forget this ever happened.' And he said, 'I'm sorry, Sadie, I just couldn't do that to her.' Apologizing for not fucking me. Oh God, the shame. And I said, trying not to be left out of being a good person, 'No, neither could I,' and he looks at me like, yeah right. He put his shirt back on and then he left. I didn't walk him to the door. I just sat on the sofa, and after he'd gone I went to the loo, and my lip was all bleeding and swollen from where he'd bitten me and my bra was grey and tatty-looking and I thought, Nice one, Sadie. Nice one.

Dear Phil,

I am afraid I shan't be able to complete the rewrite on *To Have and to Hold* as promised. In fact, as of this date, I resign from any further involvement with the screen adaptation of my memoir. It is not in my gift to prevent you from continuing with the film if you wish to do so, but I hope that, in lieu of any contractual authority, my moral claim on the fate of this project will carry some weight: I hereby put on record my request – no, my humblest appeal – that Curzon abandon its development of my book immediately. I am sufficiently revolted by the idea of *To Have and to Hold* being made into a film – whether with my script or someone else's – to actually beg you, Phil. Please. Don't do it.

No doubt you will be taken aback and not a little irritated by this volte-face on my part. But in truth, my decision is not so sudden or perverse. It is not just that this movie is destined to be a stupid movie. I have a passing acquaintance with your industry and your status within it, Phil. I understand that pointing out the certain vileness of the product is not enough, by itself, to cause you or your colleagues any consternation. Yes, the current script is a laughable piece of melodrama written by a man whose entire knowledge of the screenwriting craft is confined to what he gleaned eight years ago during a fifteen-minute scan of Syd Field's *How to Write a Screenplay*. And yes, your prospective director is an unctuous, talent-free Kraut. But in all fairness, how much anxiety can I expect these facts to cause you – a man who presided over the making of *First Tango in Rome, the Prequel*? A man who continues to protest to this day that the critics didn't really understand the picture?

So no, I won't tax you with considerations of artistic merit. Instead, let me try to give you a sense of what a bad – bad in the sense of *evil* – movie *To Have and to*

Hold would be. What wickedness and deceit it would propagate in the world. What moral pollution. (That is the second time I have had recourse to the word 'moral' in this letter, Phil. Contrary to popular myth, the authentic exercise of one's moral faculty is a rather dour and demanding business. I have seen those pictures of you and your lovely wife, in *In Style* magazine, wearing Multiple Sclerosis baseball caps at celebrity barbecues and manning the coconut shy at Pediatric Cancer fundraisers. These gestures, while touching, and no doubt personally gratifying for you, are not what I am getting at.)

I wrote *To Have and to Hold* ten years ago because I was in urgent need of cash and was able to persuade myself that financial hardship exempted me from the usual standards of good taste and sense. In the years since its publication, I have tried in various other ways to excuse my egregious action to myself. I have belittled the damage and hurt that the book caused. I have compounded my mendacity by pretending that many of the things I wrote were really true or, at least, not so very untrue. I have taken refuge in the modern notion that there is no such thing as absolute truth anyway – only a plurality of infinitely interpretable and slippery would-be truths. I have told myself that guilt is an unconstructive emotion.

All of these strategies were called into service once again at the end of last year when I agreed to sell Brad Resnick the film option to the book and then signed a contract with Curzon to write the screenplay. (It may interest you and the studio's accountants to know that the script I delivered with such impressive promptness in February was actually a draft that I wrote in 1973 shortly after arriving in Los Angeles. So the $25,000 you paid me was money for old rope.) The excuses had grown a little threadbare by this point, but they still did the job. In fact, had Hans Stempel not come on to the scene demanding script changes, and forcing me to return to 'the original material', I might have gone on evading the squalid truths underlying our deal indefinitely. But he did. And I could not.

To Have and to Hold, the book upon which your movie-to-be is based, is a lie. A great bundle of lies, actually. It would take too long and would probably not be very useful to provide a complete concordance of the book's deceits. In any case, I suspect that your own interest in the matter does not go much beyond establishing whether or not I really killed my wife. Before I satisfy your vulgar curiosity on that point, I need to explain something to you about the nature of lying.

We are taught very early, and most of us spend our lives believing, that there is a sliding scale of duplicity in life – with minor fibs and omissions at one end and big, disgraceful dishonesties at the other. Decent people, we gather, are forgiven for occasionally dabbling in the former, but are bound to strenuously resist the latter. (You've read those celebrity questionnaires, haven't you, Phil, where they ask, 'On what occasions do you lie?' and the smug reply from Julia Childs or Pavarotti or whoever always comes back, 'When I need to protect someone's feelings' or 'When the truth would be hurtful'?) Well, the truth is, duplicity doesn't lend itself to any such neat system of evaluation. Sometimes, the big, factual lies are relatively insignificant. Sometimes, the very worst sort are those dinky little omissions and diplomacies that even celebrities feel comfortable admitting to. In 1970, during an argument in our kitchen, I pushed my wife, causing her to slip, break her head on the refrigerator door handle, and die. In the opinion of both my first and second barrister, the fact that she was drunk at the time and attempting to put her fingers in my eyes did not constitute a circumstance sufficiently extenuating to convince a jury of my innocence. So I lied about the push. I lied about it in court and in my book and have continued to lie about it ever since. That's what is known as a big lie, Phil. In the eyes of the world, it's the most significant one I've ever told. But, to my mind, it is minor when compared to the string of sly rejiggings, petty avoidances and self-flattering glosses that riddle the rest of *To Have and to Hold.* You will recall that in my book (and also, I think, in the screenplay), I describe kneeling over Oona's injured body and hearing the faint, gay exclamations of a little boy in the next-door neighbour's garden. Well, there was no little boy and no gay exclamations. I put that stuff in, believing (correctly) that for the debased modern reader it would constitute a moment of thrilling pathos. Call it pretentiousness or sophistry, if you like, Phil, but for me, that tawdry little embroidery is a hundred times more damning than any lie I told about the physics of my wife's collision with the Frigidaire. And there are countless others like it.

I'm going to stop now. By the time you receive this letter, I will be away. Trying to make amends is a truly wretched business, Phil. Far better to do the right thing the first time round. Please consider what I have written, even if it seems crazy.

Yours,
Willy Muller

22

*I met Michael! I can't believe it. I had left Pearl with Pat,
next door, to go out and buy some milk. My hair was so
dirty it was sticking together in horrible clumps, and I
was wearing my really revolting blue leggings and the
plimsolls that I've worn too many times without socks so
they stink and my Aran sweater with spit-up on it. He
looked beautiful. He stared at me very hard all the time
we were talking. It was an awful, nothing conversation –
just bollocks about his work and how was my spa
thing going? Didn't ask about Pearl. An evil thought
came into my head – I wanted to throw myself at him,
just cling to him and refuse to let go. Towards the end of
the conversation, he said, 'You look very different these
days.'*

'How?' I asked. (Christ, what a sucker I am!)

*'I don't know,' he said. 'You used to have a kind of
Jewy look about you.'*

*I stared at him. 'What the fuck do you mean by that?' I
said.*

*'Oh, you know.' He smiled meanly. 'Plumper. Pinker.
Peachier.'*

'And that's how Jews look, is it?'

*He looked at me weirdly. 'What are you talking
about?' Then he began to laugh. 'No, you fool. I said
dewy, not Jewy.'*

*He carried on laughing and laughing, and I think I
went red. I used to be dewy, I thought. I used to be*

dewy. I used to be dewy and now I'm just an ugly,
worn-out old cow. He kept on laughing and laughing. I
had forgotten what a mean bastard he can be. I said I
must go now, I have to go and pick my child up, and he
didn't say anything, just looked at me. He was definitely
shitting himself. As I was walking away I had this tiny
hope that he was going to come running after me telling
me no don't go, let me come and meet her. But of course
he didn't, because nothing in life is ever like that. I
turned around once and he was walking really fast,
practically jogging to get away from me.

I could not sleep on the plane, so I spent the night roaming the aisles with my square of static blanket wrapped around me, eating little silver bags of peanuts and occasionally examining myself in the eerie orange light of the lavatory mirror. At Heathrow I stood at the baggage carousel for ten minutes before remembering that I had only brought a carry-on. Then I went outside and took a cab straight to King's Cross, feeling very clever and in charge. But at the station they said there was something wrong with the tracks, and they didn't know when service would be restored. I stood about, ridiculously crestfallen. Then I went across the street and checked myself into the King's Cross Royal. My little grey cubicle with Courtelle eiderdown and in-room tea system cost me £105. I made myself a terrible, chlorine-tasting cup of tea and watched an early morning news show. Then I fell asleep.

When I woke, it was dark outside and someone was knocking at my door.

'Who is it?' I called.

'Hello?' a female voice called back.

'What? I'm sleeping,' I said.

There was more knocking.

I got up and staggered to the door. A whey-faced woman

was standing in the hallway, looking off to her left. She was in her forties, I would guess. She blinked, as if surprised, when she saw me.

'Like some company?' she asked flatly. She was wearing a miniskirt and high red sandals that looked as if someone had been chewing on them. Her face was dirty, like a child's.

'What? No. No thank you.'

'Lick your dick for twenty-five,' she said in the same rapid monotone.

I paused, not clear in my sleep-haze whether this was an offer or an injunction.

'No. Thank you. No,' I said. Then I closed the door.

The woman kept knocking for a little while before going away. I lay awake for a long time, after that, listening to the rain that had begun popping against my window. When they were little, the girls used to have special yellow welling- ton boots for rainy days. Sadie said that their soles looked like the insides of apricots. Christ, I wish I could get this maudlin nonsense out of my head.

This morning, when I called the station, the trains were running again, so I checked out of the hotel and went back across the road. I bought some breakfast (a vicious piece of toast that punctured the roof of my mouth; more bad tea). Then I boarded the 10.25. I had bought a paper – it seemed the right thing to do – but I didn't read it. I just sat wedged in my seat behind an odd little formica desk, breathing in the orangey scent of brake rubber as we racketed past green fields and yellowing sheep and the crapped-up back gardens of poor people. A man came round once or twice, touting unpleasant snacks from a trolley, and the carriage became filled with the sound and smell of Englishman at trough.

And now I am here on the train platform, standing still in the drizzle, as the crowd flows past me. The unread newspaper is still scrunched in my fist. Oh God, I am terrified. A young woman carrying a baby shoots me a nasty look as she passes by. *Excuse me, ticket collector – there's a mad old fucker standing around up there, looking dangerous. Perhaps you ought to do something . . .* Reluctantly, I fold up the paper, put it in my bag and walk to the taxi rank. There is a long line. I stand waiting for ten minutes or so, clutching reflexively for the scrap of paper in my pocket. *It's not too late. You can turn around right now, get away from this northern shithole.*

My taxi is driven by a woman. Her hair is dyed the same colour as Art's, and this is strangely comforting to me. I show her my scrap of paper and ask if she knows where that is. Oh yes, she does, no worries. First time in Leeds? Pleasure or business? Have I come far? She doesn't seem to mind the sombre responses I dredge up. 'You look fatigued, chuck,' she says.

I get her to let me off a few doors down, to give myself time to collect myself. Collect. Collect. Now. Yes.

I walk down the street very, very slowly, gulping in cold, wet air.

The house is smaller than I remember it. The gate squeaks horribly when I push it open. I walk round to the back door and I can hear music – one of those straggle-haired women. Joni Mitchell? No, Carole King.

Tonight you're mine, completely. You give your love so sweetly . . .

The kitchen window is illuminated. I crouch like an idiot in the bushes and peer in. There is Margaret stirring something on the stove. Boy, did her arse get big. Beyond her, jigging about to the music with a small child's arhythmic solemnity, is Pearl.

Tonight the light of love is in your eyes, but will you love me tomorrow?

I am at the door now, gazing at the dimpled glass pane, trying to get my frantic old heart to slow down a little. Don't let me peg out now . . . *Only when you die do you run out of chances to be good*. I am sweating like Nixon. I wonder if she will sense my fear. I check my breath – children hate old men's cigarette smell. I am fine. No rosebud, but fine. I am a mad old man. No I'm not. I open the door and walk in.

'Hello, Margaret,' I hear myself saying, from a long way away. The room is filled with the smell of baking. Margaret is staring at me with large, frightened eyes. Pearl has stopped dancing. My shirt is sticking to my back. I smile at her. No, that won't do. I kneel down before her, like a knight plighting his troth. 'Hello,' I say, looking into her serious, little-girl eyes. 'Can you guess who I am?'

Acknowledgements

For their moral support and good advice, I am very thankful to Larry Konner, Lucy, Bruno, Miranda and Emily Heller, Pat Kavanagh, Richard Duguid, Hilton Als, Claudia Shear and Colin Robinson. I also owe a special debt of gratitude to Roger Thornham, who was no help whatsoever in the writing of this book but who was – and is – invaluable to me in every other way.

ZOE HELLER

NOTES ON A SCANDAL

From the first day that the beguiling Sheba Hart joins the staff of St George's, history teacher Barbara Covett is convinced that she has found a kindred spirit. Barbara's loyalty to her new friend is passionate and unstinting and when Sheba is discovered having an illicit affair with one of her young pupils, Barbara quickly elects herself as Sheba's chief defender. But all is not as at first it seems in this dark story and, as Sheba will soon discover, a friend can be just as treacherous as any lover.

'Fascinating, brilliant, horribly addictive' *Guardian*

'Superbly gripping' *Daily Telegraph*

'Deliciously sinister' *Daily Mail*

'Brilliant, nasty, gripping' Zadie Smith, *Observer*

Shortlisted for the 2003 Man Booker Prize